Follow Andrina Adamo's dancing career through these
new editions of the Drina ballet books.

**The Drina books:**

# Drina Dances in New York

by
Jean Estoril

SIMON & SCHUSTER
YOUNG BOOKS

Cover artwork by Kevin Jones
Cover design by Terence Kingston
Illustrations by Jenny Sanders

First published in Great Britain by Hodder & Stoughton Ltd
Second edition published in Great Britain by MacDonald & Co
(Publishers) Ltd

This edition published in 1992 by
Simon & Schuster Young Books
Campus 400
Maylands Avenue
Hemel Hempstead HP2 7EZ

Printed and bound at Cox & Wyman Ltd, Reading, Berkshire,
England

British Library Cataloguing in Publication Data available

ISBN: 0-7500-1265-X

# CONTENTS

# BOOK ONE
## Ballet at Sea

# 1

# Drina's Choice

"**L**ondon looks just the same," said Drina, gazing out eagerly as the taxi sped down Whitehall.

Her grandfather, Mr Chester, laughed. "Would you expect it to look different? We were only in Scotland a short time."

Drina pushed back her straight, almost black hair and frowned thoughtfully at Big Ben.

"I suppose not, but such a lot seems to have happened to *me* since I saw London last. It still seems like a dream – that I danced Little Clara in *Casse Noisette* at the Edinburgh Festival. And think! Only last night we were watching the Military Tattoo on the Castle Esplanade. When that lone piper stood on the battlements, with everywhere else dark, I could have – " But she bit back the words "I could have cried," because that was the kind of remark that always annoyed her grandmother.

Mrs Chester had brought Drina up since she was only eighteen months old and she had done her best to turn her grandchild into a well-balanced and sensible girl, for Mrs Chester disliked and slightly feared "temperament" and too much emotion. She had never ceased to regret the fact that Drina was so easily carried away by any kind of beauty.

The taxi swung round Parliament Square and a very short time later the Chesters and Drina were going up in the lift to their flat in a big modern block just off Millbank. When Mr Chester opened the front door there was a pile of letters on the mat and he looked through them hastily while his wife opened doors and glanced critically about to see that all was well.

"Business letters, most of them. Three postcards for you, Drina."

Mr Chester read his letters and became very thoughtful. He said presently, "I'm afraid I've got to go to New York very soon. There's a Conference and I thought that Carter was going, but he writes to say that he's got to go into hospital for observation."

"You won't fly?" Mrs Chester asked quickly.

"No, I'll go by sea, but it means leaving next week. I shall have to sort out my clothes."

Mrs Chester sighed again. Really, after a pleasant holiday, life was turning out rather difficult. "Can't someone else go? You're not at all strong and New York is such a tiring place – "

"I think I must go, and I'm much better than I was. And I should be glad to see New York again. I always liked it."

Drina stared at him. "I didn't know you'd ever been."

"Oh, yes, many times, but mostly before you were born," he told her. "I used to go on business, and then there was Betsy – "

"When she danced there, do you mean?"

"She often danced there and she had many friends. We went twice to see her dance at the Metropolitan Opera House and to stay with people she knew."

"Goodness! I didn't realise that." And Drina tried to imagine them both in that, to her, almost fabulous city. New York! She had seen Milan and Genoa and that had seemed wonderful enough, but New York –

Drina's mother, who had once, long ago, been ordinary, red-haired Betsy Chester, had turned into the great dancer, Elizabeth Ivory, and Drina's greatest – almost her only – wish was that she might be a dancer, too. That was why it had been so wonderful to have the chance of going to Edinburgh with the Igor Dominick Company, while she was still only a Junior.

Drina went thoughtfully to her room to unpack her cases. She was just changing into something cooler, since the September day was very warm, when Ilonka Lorencz arrived.

Ilonka was one of Drina's friends at the Dominick Ballet School. Her father and mother kept a restaurant called "The Golden Zither" and her sister Terza was in the Dominick Company. Terza had written a best-selling book about her escape from Lynzonia, *Diary of a Dancer*.

Ilonka was in high spirits, delighted to see Drina again. "You must tell me about Edinburgh! It was so exciting to see you on television as Little Clara. Oh, Drina – "

"I will tell, of course. It was all wonderful, and Rose enjoyed it, too, as understudy. But things have been happening since we got back. Grandfather's going off to New York. Have *you* any news?"

"But yes. Terza has nearly finished her second book, *Dancer at the Dominick,* and Blane and Marshton say they will publish it in the spring. But the play of *Diary of a Dancer* is to be delayed. The third act is to be rewritten and then there are other difficulties."

"What a shame! But I know it's going to be a wonderful play. Have you seen anyone from the Dominick?"

Ilonka nodded, her small, heart-shaped face looking

mischievous. "I saw Queenie Rothington in Piccadilly. She stuck her nose in the air so high that she could not see where she was going. She was so nearly run over by a taxi."

"One day she'll fall flat on her back," Drina remarked, for, in company with many of the other students at the Dominick, she disliked the unpleasant girl. "She won't have Daphne Daniety as an ally next term. But she'll have Christine Gifford from Chalk Green instead, and together they'll be terrible." Drina had suffered much from Christine Gifford while at the Dominick Residential School in the Chilterns and was really thoroughly dismayed to think of meeting her again at the London school in Red Lion Square. For Christine was now fifteen and was being transferred to London.

They chatted on about Dominick matters until Ilonka had to go, and, after an early dinner, Mrs Chester suggested that Drina should go to bed.

Drina obeyed without argument, but she could not sleep for a long time. She had so much to think about. All the excitement of Edinburgh already seemed far away and she was caught up again in thoughts of the Dominick and her friends.

Drina got up late next morning, worn out after her long day. She looked sleepily round her own little room, giving an affectionate glance at the Degas reproduction above the pillow and the Utrillo print on the opposite wall. It was nice to be home, with the knowledge that the autumn term at the Dominick lay ahead. It was September 9th and school started again on the following Tuesday, the 15th.

While she was eating a late breakfast, her grandmother said, "By the way, we've been making plans while you were asleep."

"Oh?"

"Your grandfather has arranged for me to go to New York with him. He's booked a large double cabin on the *Queen of the Atlantic* for next Thursday, and they are holding a small one for you. Of course I suppose you could go to stay with Miss Whiteway or one of your friends at the Dominick, but it seems a pity for you to miss a wonderful experience. You love travel, after all, and – "

Drina had gone very white.

"Granny, what do you mean? Me go to New York? I never dreamed – I couldn't ever imagine – "

"It would only be for a short time. Under a fortnight there and the sea trip both ways. Say three and a half weeks to a month. The *Queen of the Atlantic* is a very fast ship. We'll be there early the following Tuesday morning."

"But what about the Dominick and my work? I couldn't possibly – it's the beginning of the school year – "

Mrs Chester said patiently:

"It's up to you, Drina. You must make your own choice. We'd like to take you with us, and surely, when you've even worked in the holidays, it couldn't do much harm to your dancing to miss a few weeks?"

"Oh, dear! Isn't life difficult? What an awful choice to have to make, Granny!"

"I don't know that it's so awful. I think you're a very lucky girl to have such a chance. And your mother loved New York."

"I should love it, too. It looks – it looks unbelievable, like a dream place."

"I assure you that it's very real. But you'll have to make up your mind by this evening. We'll have to confirm your cabin and get some travellers' cheques for you. You'll want some dollars to buy presents and so on."

"You make it sound so easy," said Drina, bitterly torn. New York! In less than a fortnight she might actually be there, might actually see the city outspread below; might walk along Fifth Avenue and stand under the flags in the Rockefeller Plaza. Above all, she would sail in in the morning, seeing the tapering buildings looming up like coloured lupins in the breaking mist.

But over the years she had formed the almost unchangeable habit of work, and her dancing came first, even before wonderful trips to America. And her conscience told her that she should not – could not – miss the first weeks of the new term.

Presently she took her shoulder-bag and a sweater and went out to try and get her tumbled thoughts into some kind of order. Walking along the Embankment in the sunshine, with Waterloo Bridge looping the river just ahead, she felt torn as she had scarcely ever been before. Could it really matter to miss a few weeks at the Dominick? But then she pictured Queenie Rothington's triumphant face if she fell behind in her work and it seemed certain that she would have to turn her back on this wonderful chance.

Almost without being aware of it her footsteps took her towards Kingsway and soon she was approaching Red Lion Square. But what good would it do to stand there and look at the Dominick School? It was still holidaytime and everyone would be far away. She was therefore very surprised to see Miss Volonaise's car parked in the square and her heart leaped with hope. Madam would tell her what to do.

The entrance hall of the Dominick was deserted and Drina glanced, as always, towards her mother's portrait and her ballet shoes in the glass case. Elizabeth Ivory

had loved New York, but it had caused her death, however indirectly. She had died when Drina was only a baby when the plane in which she was travelling to the United States had crashed into the sea. Suddenly Drina was sharply relieved that her grandparents were not flying, though most people seemed to regard it as a perfectly safe way of travelling.

Marianne Volonaise, was in her office and the door was half-open. Drina, seeing her figure at the desk, knocked gently and then obeyed the order to "come in".

"Good gracious, Drina! What are you doing here? Do you want me?"

Drina flushed, feeling suddenly shy, for she had not seen Miss Volonaise since that Sunday morning in Edinburgh when Mr Dominick had told her that the Directors of the Dominick Ballet School and Company had guessed her secret.

Until recently Drina had managed to keep the secret of her mother's greatness from nearly everyone. She had sturdily, almost grimly, decided that she would succeed on her own, without the help of Elizabeth Ivory's name. That was partly why she was always called Drina Adams instead of her real name, Andrina Adamo, for people might remember that Ivory had been married to an Italian businessman with the unusual surname of Adamo. However, Mr Dominick and Marianne Volonaise had discovered the truth while they were all in Edinburgh. They had promised to keep the secret and Drina was sure that they would keep their word.

As Miss Volonaise gazed at her now in surprise, Drina hesitated, then poured out her dilemma. Marianne Volonaise listened carefully, her eyes on the anxious, attractive face.

"Oh dear! I see. And I know you hate missing any of your classes. But you've worked in the holidays. Don't you think that might make up for it?"

"Granny said that. And I should so like to see New York. But if you think it would harm my dancing – "

The Director of the School laughed. "I don't think a few weeks' absence could possibly do much damage. It might even improve your dancing. All new experiences help, you know, and you are the sort of person to whom other countries mean a great deal. When would you have to go?"

"We sail next Thursday, but Granny says they'll probably go down to Southampton the day before and spend the night there. The boat trains leave very early and she doesn't like an early start."

"So that would only give you one day at the Dominick. Still, it would be better to come in on the Tuesday and learn about your classes and get your timetable."

"Oh! Then do you really think I can go?"

"Of course I think you can go. And it will give you a chance to see the Metropolitan Opera House, perhaps."

"Oh, I do hope so!"

"Your mother danced there, of course," Miss Volonaise added, searching her face. "You'll be interested in it on that account."

"Yes, I – I will, of course."

"Have a good time, Drina, and don't worry any more."

Drina almost danced out into Red Lion Square. It was all right! It was certain to be all right if Miss Volonaise said so.

"Everything lovely happens to me," she told herself, as she walked back towards the river. "Granny's right; I *am* terribly lucky."

As she hurried home her thoughts raced ahead and she began to plan all that she must do.

# 2
# Jenny Pilgrim
# in Trouble

Next morning Mr Chester brought Drina a letter.

"It looks as if it's from Jenny Pilgrim," he said, seeing the Willerbury postmark.

Drina took the letter eagerly, for, even more than Rose, Jenny was her best friend. They only met a few times a year, but that made no difference at all to their relationship.

"Oh, good! She only wrote once to Edinburgh."

Standing by the window in her own room, from which she could just see the River Thames and Lambeth Bridge, she opened Jenny's letter. Her wild cry two minutes later almost made Mrs Chester drop the electric kettle.

"What's the matter?" she called. "Have you hurt yourself?"

Drina appeared in the kitchen doorway. Her face, sun-tanned after the long summer holidays, was suddenly alarmingly white, her dark eyes were wide and distressed and the hand that held Jenny's letter shook slightly.

"Granny, it's terrible!"

Mrs Chester plugged in the kettle and switched it on before she spoke. She was by then convinced that it was just another of Drina's unnecessary emotional outbursts.

"Pull yourself together, Drina dear, and tell me quietly. I'm sure there's no need to look so tragic. I sometimes wonder if you'll ever get more balanced. After all, you'll be fifteen in only a few weeks' time – "

"But, Granny, it really is awful. Jenny said a while ago – she said that her mother and her father seemed worried, and I knew she was worried, too. But – "

"Has something happened to Mr Pilgrim's business?" Mr Chester asked.

Drina spun round, very startled. "How did you know? How *could* you know?"

"These things get about," he said slowly. "I had heard a rumour a while ago, but I hoped it was untrue."

"The firm's gone bankrupt," Drina told him, still rather tremulously. "When everything is sorted out Mr Pilgrim will have almost nothing. He won't even have a job. And Jenny – "

"That *is* tragic news," her grandfather said, looking very distressed. "And with so many children, none of them earning – "

"Poor Mrs Pilgrim!" said Mrs Chester compassionately.

"But what about poor Jenny?" Drina demanded, staring at them with eyes so dark that they looked quite black. "It's just as though I'd been told I could never dance again." In fact, she had once been told just that, when her grandparents had decided that dancing was bad for her, and the memory was still a bitter one. She had fought and won, but Jenny –

"Jenny's a sensible girl," said her grandmother, not understanding. "I feel sure that she can shoulder anything. She'll be a great help and comfort to her mother."

"But, Granny, don't you see? Jenny feels about farming as I do about dancing. It's the only thing in the world that she's absolutely sure about – that she *must* go farming. She was going to stay on at school for another two years, at least, and then she wanted to go to an agricultural college. It wasn't going to be easy, because there are all the others, and Philip is still training to be a doctor. But she never really doubted that she'd manage it."

"And now, you think, it will be quite impossible?"

Drina opened the letter and turned the pages.

"She just says at the end: 'All this will put paid to my going farming. I can't face it yet, but I shall have to sooner or later. Oh, Drina, how shall I bear it?' "

"Jenny will bear it. She's made of sterner stuff, and, in any case, I've never thought farming a very suitable occupation – "

"It's suitable for Jenny. She knows everything about farm life already, only she'd have to go to College to get a proper job. She can't even just go and live on her uncle's farm, because they may be selling up and going to Australia." Drina thought for a moment and then added, "Granny, I've got to go to Willerbury. I've got to be there. I can't leave her to face it all alone!"

Mrs Chester was frowning as she put tea in the pot. "Are you sure they'd want you at a time like this? I really don't think – oh, well, don't distress yourself again. Sit down and have a quiet cup of tea. And it would be most inconvenient for you to go just now, with our American trip so close."

Drina did sit down, and drank the tea; she even absently ate some toast, but her thoughts were far away and her mind was made up. Mrs Chester saw her face and told herself with a sigh that Drina would go her own way. Still so small and childish in appearance, she was developing mentally all the time, and if she thought she must go to Jenny it was probably not the faintest use arguing.

Soon afterwards Drina asked her grandmother's permission and then went towards the telephone.

"But if you go you are only to stay one night," Mrs Chester said firmly after her retreating back. "You'll never settle until you've seen Jenny, I know, but you must be quite firm about it being a very short visit. It will be a very distressing time for them all and they won't want a visitor – "

Drina, however, did not believe that the Pilgrims would regard her as a visitor, and Jenny's cry of relief when she suggested going to Willerbury was proof enough that she was wanted.

"Oh, Drina, how I have missed you! Yes, come tomorrow on that fast morning train. Well, if your Granny insists on only one night there's nothing we can do about it, but just the sight of you – "

"But what about your mother – "

"Oh, Mother wants you to come. She regards you as almost one of the family – " Jenny's voice sounded much as usual, but Drina knew her too well not to recognise the strain in it.

"I am, of course. Oh, Jenny, I *am* so sorry about it all!" In Willerbury Jenny made a sound that might have been a snort or a stifled sob. Then she said:

"I suppose we'll work it out. More when I see you. I'll meet you. 'Bye!" And the line went dead.

That evening Drina telephoned Rose Conway and her friend was wildly envious to hear of her good fortune.

"Oh, Drina, New York! How – how extraordinary! I

can't imagine even seeing Paris." For Rose's family was quite poor and even to see Edinburgh, and to stay in a big hotel with the Chesters and Drina, had been a startling new experience.

"I can't believe I shall ever really get there. But Miss Volonaise says it's all right to go. I shall miss nearly a month of term."

"You'll miss dear Queenie and Christine, anyway. Chalk Green will be a better place without Christine." Rose had a scholarship to the Residential School in the Chilterns and she had suffered even more than Drina from Christine's supercilious, unfriendly ways. "By the way, my father had a letter from Mr Dominick, and I'm to stay on at Chalk Green until Easter."

"Oh, *Rose*! I thought you'd be back in London after Christmas!"

"So did I, but Mr Dominick says it will be better if I stay in the country until the spring. You know I went because I was anaemic and not very well."

"But you're fine now, surely?"

"Of course I am," said Rose robustly. "But we can't argue about it and I do love Chalk Green."

Drina and her grandmother settled down to making plans. There was so much to arrange, lists to be compiled, and so on.

"I expect it will be quite warm in New York," Mrs Chester said, frowning over Drina's summer clothes. "They've had a very, very hot summer by all accounts. But you'll need sweaters and a warm coat for the ship, and dresses for evening, of course. I think we'd better buy you a couple of new ones, if there's time, or we can get them in New York and you must manage on the outward journey. You've got the red dress that was bought in Milan, and there's your white one and the old turquoise blue one. Luckily you don't grow much –"

"No." Drina glanced at herself in the looking-glass. She still looked no more than twelve and it was beginning to be a slight grief to her. To be nearly fifteen and to look like a child was really very annoying. "Could I have some proper evening shoes, please, Granny?"

"You've got your silver slippers."

"But they're so flat. If I had some with heels I'd look taller."

"And break your neck most likely," Mrs Chester said resignedly. Drina had recently been demanding more adult clothes and she was not sure that she liked it.

It was clear that things were very wrong with Jenny, as Drina knew the moment she saw her friend.

She spent the journey with a book unopened in her lap, staring out – once London was left behind – at the September countryside. Most of the corn was in now and the stubble fields, with here and there still a bright fringe of poppies, glowed under the very blue sky. As yet the woods were still untouched by autumn and, as the express sped through part of her beloved Chilterns, the beechwoods rolled away thick and green over the softly rounded hills. But soon the Chilterns were left behind and the train sped towards the flatter country of Warwickshire.

Jenny was on the platform when the express drew up in Willerbury and Drina's first startled thought was that she looked much older and just as though she had been ill. Jenny was tall and fair and inclined to be fat, but she had certainly lost weight since their last meeting only a few weeks ago. She had dark circles under her eyes and her hair, usually so crisp and bright, was limp and dull.

"Hullo, my duck!" Jenny gave her usual greeting, but she did not kiss her friend as she sometimes did. She held out her hand for Drina's small case and added rather rapidly, as though for once she felt ill at ease, "You must be simply starving. I told Mother we'd have lunch in the town. There's that nice place, 'The Singing Kettle,' quite near the station."

Drina nodded, also smitten with unusual shyness. She and Jenny almost regarded themselves as sisters and it frightened her to feel so awkward and inadequate – with Jenny of all people! She hoped, as she followed Jenny out of the station and into the familiar square, that the feeling would not last.

It was three years since she had lived in Willerbury, but she had visited Jenny often enough to feel that she still knew it well. Just outside 'The Singing Kettle' they came face to face with Mark Playford, a good-looking dark-haired boy of fifteen, whom Drina had known in the old days at the Selswick Dancing School. He had recently been accepted by the Dominick School in London and would be starting there the following week. He was a fine dancer for his age and fully intended to make ballet his career.

Mark greeted them warmly, but said at once, to Drina's relief, that he had to hurry home. He had just come out to get the fish for lunch.

"But I'll see you next week, Drina," he said, with a slightly rueful grin.

"Yes, and you will like it, you know, Mark," Drina assured him, though she knew that he was going to find the change to a different school rather difficult.

"Drina will hold your hand at the Dominick. You know she promised," said Jenny.

Mark grinned again. "I don't say it won't be welcome." He waved the parcel of fish and went on his way, and Drina asked hesitantly:

"Does he – know about you?"

Jenny shrugged.

"I've no doubt the whole town knows. You can't keep that kind of thing dark, especially when it's such a well-known firm. But most people have been very tactful. That almost makes it worse," she added, as she led the way into 'The Singing Kettle' and moved cautiously between the crowded tables to one in a corner. It was a little cut off from the rest, in a rather dark alcove.

When they had given their order Jenny suddenly slipped her hand under the table and squeezed Drina's fingers.

"It's all right. Don't look so stricken. I know I'm not myself, but I really am most dreadfully glad to see you. I'll talk when I get going, but I've been closed up like a clam. I feel tense all over; even my neck aches."

But they did not really talk until they had finished lunch and were sitting on a secluded seat in the little park near Jenny's home. Then suddenly she seemed to find words and poured out the whole story of the anxious weeks and the final breaking of the news she had somehow been expecting, though she had only had hints to go on.

"I feel so desperately sorry for Father. That's really the worst thing about it. It isn't his fault and he's done everything he can to see that as few people as possible suffer. At least, though, he's had the offer of a job. We heard this morning, and that *is* something, though it's only a clerk's job."

"The boys have been splendid. The young ones have been as good as anything, though they were upset when they heard that they'd have to change their schools. School fees are impossible of course, though Donny and Bill's headmaster has been very good and has let us off paying next term's fees. Roger and David will go comprehensive, but we haven't had time to sort it all out yet, and Philip wanted to give up all idea of being a doctor, but we had a family meeting and decided that he *must* keep on. He's got his grant and he can work during his vacations. I'm going to the Grossdale Comprehensive for a term or two, until I'm sixteen. I'm taking classes in shorthand, typing and book-keeping. And a friend of Dad's is really great. He's promised me a job in his insurance office just as soon as I can leave school." Jenny's tone was carefully casual, showing none of the despair she felt over her changed circumstances.

"They shouldn't have asked you to do it."

"They didn't ask. I'm not a baby; sometimes I feel like a grown woman, and when the family is in trouble I can't insist on going my own selfish way. Actually Mother wanted to write and beg one of the aunts to help me, so that I could stay on at school and then go to an agricultural college. But I won't take charity and I won't be treated like a child. It's my own decision. I must earn if I can."

"But it will kill you." Drina felt that she had never seen the real Jenny before. This set-faced, decisive girl was nothing like the light-hearted friend who had always seemed so casual and easy-going.

"People don't die so easily," said Jenny.

"Granny says that sometimes to me. When – when I said once that I should die if I couldn't dance – "

"But one part of me feels dead already," Jenny confessed in a sudden rush, and her lips trembled. "I've faced it all and I know what I'm doing. And shorthand typists earn good money nowadays. If things improve I can start saving up and I may get to agricultural college in the end, though probably rather late. Still, I'm not even thinking of that."

"I think you're the bravest person I've ever met," said Drina, and meant it with all her heart.

"Rubbish! Think of Terza and Ilonka Lorencz and all they suffered. They lost their home and country and everything they'd ever had. I've still got Father and Mother and the boys and you. I'm young and healthy and a few years of doing something that's against my nature won't matter – "

"Oh, but I wish you needn't do it at all."

Jenny plucked a leaf off a nearby lilac bush and shredded it minutely.

"I wish it hadn't had to happen – for Father's and Mother's sake as well as mine – but it *has* happened, so that's that. And now I feel better. Tell me about Edinburgh and all you've been doing, and do try not to look tragic in front of Mother. I'm trying so hard to make her believe that everything's all right. It doesn't work, of course, but I go on pretending."

Drina did her best to obey, but she was further shaken when she saw how old and ill Mrs Pilgrim looked. The four boys, however, looked much the same as usual and they greeted her eagerly, for they too looked on her as almost one of the family. Philip had a holiday job and was not there, and, somewhat to her relief, Mr Pilgrim was out.

Though everyone tried to behave as usual it was a considerable strain, and Drina was glad when the television was turned on. At eight o'clock there was a coincidence that pleased her very much and for a time it made her forget the Pilgrims' troubles. This was a documentary about Manhattan, beautifully filmed, with some splendid shots of the most dramatic aspects. Drina gasped as the cameras travelled up the World Trade Towers and then showed views from the top: Rockefeller Plaza, then the views from the RCA building ... Lincoln Centre ... Central Park. The final shots were of the park under snow.

It seemed amazing that in a few days she would actually be there.

The next day Drina parted from Jenny with a heavy heart, hating it all the more because she was really powerless to help her friend.

"But don't worry," said Jenny, looking up at her from the platform just before the train left. "We'll all manage, and I really do feel better for having seen you. Have a wonderful time in New York."

# 3

# One Day at the Dominick

The last days of the holidays passed busily and pleasantly, on the whole, though Mrs Chester was harassed at times and vowed that they would never be ready for New York in time. Drina had so much to do that for once she scarcely gave a thought to the new term at the Dominick, but Tuesday morning found her putting on her red dress – the weather was still warm enough for the summer uniform – and setting off with her little case for Red Lion Square. In the case she carried shoes, practice clothes, a towel, and one of her dearest possessions, a small black cat called Hansl. Hansl had been Elizabeth Ivory's own mascot and she had left it behind when she set off on that last fatal journey. Drina never went far without Hansl and the black cat would certainly go to America on the *Queen of the Atlantic*.

Everywhere, as she reached the square, were girls in scarlet dresses and boys in grey suits and red ties. Ilonka came flying towards her, her dark curls bobbing on her shoulders.

"Oh, Drina, I shall miss you so! I wish that you were not going to New York!"

"But think of all the exciting things I shall have to tell you," said Drina, gazing ahead to where two girls were standing on the steps of the Dominick School. Queenie and Christine, and they had got together already! Their heads were close and they were giggling about something.

"There's Mark!" Drina cried suddenly, and quickened her steps until she had caught up with the newcomer. "Mark! You've got here, then? This is Ilonka Lorencz."

Mark, looking slightly at bay, said a polite "How do you do?" to Ilonka, who smiled warmly at him. Ilonka liked English boys, especially ones with kind, good-looking faces.

"What a crowd!" Mark groaned. "I feel more like turning tail."

"Oh, don't. There's no need. Look! Here's Jan Williams. He's in our class, and you'll be in the one above, I suppose, but he'll tell you where to go and introduce you to some of the older boys. Jan, this is Mark Playford," she said hastily, to the sensible-looking boy who was one of her special friends at the Dominick. "He's new and doesn't know where to go. We used to know each other at Willerbury. He knows Miss Selswick, anyway." For their old teacher, Janetta Selswick, had sold her school some time before and was now teaching and advising at the Dominick.

Mark went off with Jan, looking somewhat more cheerful, and on their way to the cloakrooms Ilonka and Drina came face to face with Igor Dominick Junior, a handsome boy of nearly sixteen, with long dark lashes and a slightly superior air. This air of being better than most people had made him very unpopular during his first term, but now he was on fairly friendly terms with most people. Drina eyed him coolly, however, and gave a rather stiff little smile.

"Hullo, Igor! You got back from Edinburgh, then?"

"But yes," he said cheerfully. "And now I hear we are to lose you, Drina."

"Only for a month," she said, and went on with Ilonka, who was looking a bit puzzled.

"But, Drina, you were so cold and dignified! I thought you and Igor were friends since Italy!"

"I thought so, too," Drina said grimly. "But he was pretty horrid in Edinburgh. He scarcely looked at Rose and me because he had a French cousin staying with him – silly, pretty thing she was, too! It will take me some time to feel the same about him, if I ever do." Her feelings had been more hurt than she had ever admitted, because she really had thought of Igor as a friend to be trusted. It had cut her deeply to be almost totally ignored and, to add insult to injury, Igor had come up to her on the last Sunday in Edinburgh and behaved just as though nothing had happened. Marie had gone and he had taken it for granted that he could be friends with Drina Adams again.

Until recently the new term at the Dominick had started merely with ballet classes, but now things had been changed and there was a full school day. But the ballet classes came first and, back at the *barre* in the big, light studio, Drina could scarcely believe that this was just one solitary day at the Dominick. Regret swept through her in a wave and immediately her body stiffened and she did the wrong movement – very badly, too. The teacher noticed at once.

"What is it, Drina? Not concentrating? I expected better from you, especially after that very good Little Clara in Edinburgh. Now *plié* in the second position – "

Drina gave her mind to the familiar exercises and was conscious of the sense of well-being that generally filled her when she was working. The class went on, with the

teacher frequently regretting the length of the summer holidays.

"Meryl, are your *port de bras* usually as bad as that? Ilonka, pull in your tail, child, and stop looking out of the window. Queenie, haven't you practised *at all* during the holidays?"

"Yes, heaps," said Queenie sulkily. She expected nothing but praise.

"One would not have thought so."

But no further criticism came Drina's way and the feeling of well-being continued until she was on her way back to the cloakroom to change into ordinary clothes. Just one day at the Dominick – it wasn't right!

"Perhaps I needn't go to America, after all," she thought. "I really ought to stay and get on with my work. Perhaps I could telephone Grandfather – "

But there was no chance to do anything of the kind; really no chance to think coherently at all about anything but the making of timetables and the listing and arranging of new books. Her desk was beside Ilonka's, as usual, and she wondered fleetingly what would happen when Rose came back to the Dominick. Once they had always shared a desk.

Since things were disorganised at the flat she stayed for lunch in the Dominick canteen, but even then there was no time for thought, for there was Mark to talk to and try to make feel at home, as well as Meryl, Jill, Betty, Bella and many of the others, who were all anxious to tell holiday experiences and to hear about Edinburgh.

Queenie, sitting with Christine, said nastily into a brief silence, "I hear that Drina was late for one performance and Rose had to go on. I bet everyone was mad!"

"As a matter of fact they weren't," Drina said mildly. "I felt terrible, but Mr Dominick was very nice about it, and it did give Rose a chance to dance."

"I should never miss a performance," said Queenie, "After all, it's unprofessional conduct. But then my mother was Beryl Bertram – "

"And mine was Elizabeth Ivory," Drina breathed, but so low that no one could possibly have heard. For a wild moment she wished she could see their faces if she made the announcement aloud. But of course she would never do it.

Rose had never been able to understand why Drina didn't boast about her famous mother, especially when people like Queenie boasted about *their* mothers who had been dancers. But Drina had always answered, with a firmly held chin:

"I don't want people to know. If I'm good it'll be all right, anyway, and if I'm bad it would only make it worse to have people know that my mother was Ivory."

"*And* Drina's going to miss a whole month of term – " That was Christine, her face even more spiteful than Queenie's. Queenie was very sure of her own importance and very jealous of Drina, but she was not quite so unpleasant as Christine Gifford, who had been greatly disliked at Chalk Green.

"Yes. She's going to New York. I'm sure we all envy her," Jan said clearly, pausing with a cup of coffee held suggestively over Christine's head. She ducked and glared at him.

"Catherine Colby and Peter Bernoise are going to America soon, so I heard," Jan remarked, putting down the coffee quite safely. "Perhaps they'll be on your ship."

"To dance?" Drina asked eagerly. She deeply admired the Dominick ballerina and her good-looking husband, principal male dancer of the Company.

"I don't know. I just read somewhere that they're going this week."

Drina said to Ilonka as they went back to their classroom. "Do you know, I feel terrible! I wish I wasn't going to America. I know it was the wrong decision, in spite of Miss Volonaise. I shall feel guilty every moment of the time."

"But that is silly."

"It may be, but I shall." And Drina went home in a restless frame of mind, thinking of life at the Dominick going on without her. But she had too much sense to confess her feelings to her grandmother, though Mrs Chester, sensing that all was not quite well, thought her overtired and insisted on early bed.

The next morning they finished the packing and did all the last minute things and then caught an afternoon train for Southampton. Drina's spirits were still unaccountably low, and her thoughts kept flying back to the Dominick. By the time she returned, so much might have happened, though she tried to convince herself that life would go on there smoothly, with no special excitements and changes.

They were to spend the night at a large white-painted hotel in the High Street, and both her grandparents decided to rest before dinner. Drina set off to explore a little, for she had never been to Southampton before. The sound of ships' hooters led her without difficulty towards the docks and presently she could see the water and, over the masts and funnels of smaller ships, a vast white ship loomed. The *Queen of the Atlantic* certainly! No other ship could be as large as that.

She stood on the corner, with her hair blowing in the warm wind, and excitement came flooding back, and with it a feeling of utter incredulity. She, Drina Adams, was to sail away from England, not merely to France, so near across the Channel, but to America.

On the way back she suddenly had an overpowering

desire to telephone Jenny, and she entered a call-box and rang the familiar Willerbury number. Jenny herself answered.

"Oh, Drina, how nice to hear you! Where are you? Southampton?"

"Yes, and I've just seen the *Queen of the Atlantic*. She's a palace, Jenny: I know I shall get lost in her. I *wish* you were coming, too."

Jenny sighed, then laughed. She sounded more herself, as Drina noted with deep relief.

"Not this time. Life is real and very earnest. But I shall think of you all the time, especially on Tuesday morning."

"Don't forget that we'll be five hours behind you."

"Behind? Oh, I see. I suppose you put the clocks back as you go. I'll remember."

"But how are *you*?"

"Not so bad. I've started at the Grossdale. There's quite a nice crowd. Most of the boys are a bit spotty and unhealthy-looking, but – "

"Oh, dear!"

"But there's one called Timothy who's keen on climbing and he goes youth-hostelling in the holidays. He's about two feet taller than me!"

"He must be a giant, then."

"Not quite. I like him."

Drina hung up with her admiration for Jenny greatly increased. To be able to be cheerful when things had gone so very wrong seemed to her the height of courage.

Guilt over missing the Dominick was still slightly with her the next morning as they sped towards the docks in a taxi. But the sun shone so warmly and brightly, and it was so thrilling to see the vast dark Customs' Shed and to glimpse the ship through openings in its side, that once more excitement overwhelmed her.

They went up in a lift and found themselves in a large, bright hall, where music played and people bustled anxiously about. There were flowers in tubs outside the windows and once more she could see the *Queen of the Atlantic*. Mr Chester was very calm and businesslike, but Mrs Chester was, for once, inclined to fuss. Was he sure that their luggage would be all right while they waited for their turn with the emigration people? Had Drina got the small case safely? Oh, dear, it *was* hot and she had made a mistake in wearing her new shoes!

Drina said little, for her ears were alert for all the American voices: people returning home after a summer in Europe. There were quite a number of children and young people and she eyed them curiously, supposing them to be seasoned travellers.

"Have your passport ready, Drina," said her grandfather in her ear, and then they were at one of the small tables and Mr Chester was explaining that his was only a short business trip and showing the return tickets.

A few minutes later they were going up the long covered gangway and were actually on the ship, following a white-clad steward along a broad, high passage. Mr and Mrs Chester's cabin was an outside one, very large and beautifully furnished, and with a bathroom. Drina stood staring about in awe and astonishment, for she had never thought that any ship could be so splendid.

Her own cabin was further along the same corridor and was an inside one and very much smaller. Her grandfather, who had accompanied her, looked round doubtfully.

"This was the best I could get, as it's a busy time. Sure you'll be all right?"

"Oh, of course. It's wonderful." And Drina was already poking into the wardrobe, examining the life jacket that hung there. There was a telephone on the dressing-table (how astonishing, if she liked she could still speak to someone in London!), and there were also all sorts of interesting switches and gadgets.

"Then I should unpack and go up on deck," Mr Chester said. "We sail at twelve, so you've got plenty of time to settle in."

At twelve o'clock Drina stood high on the Boat Deck, the sun hot on her shoulders. The gangways had been removed and the great ship's siren made a noise that sent a wild thrill of excitement up her spine. Leaning on the rail, she looked across at all the watchers on the high balcony and thought:

"I couldn't bear to stand there and wave us away. I'm glad I'm here." And tears of excitement and disbelief pricked her eyes. It was a good thing that Mrs Chester was not near to see her emotion, for she would certainly not have thought that a short trip to New York warranted any kind of tears. But it was so thrilling to be there on the deck of a great liner, and there was another side to it, too. For it gave her a slight insight into what it must be like to be leaving England for a long time, perhaps forever.

She heard a young woman saying that she had married an American only the week before.

"I love him and I suppose it's going to be wonderful. But I don't know when I shall see England again."

Drina gripped the rail as the space between ship and quay widened rapidly.

"I shall come back soon," she thought thankfully.

"I'll come back to Jenny and Rose and Ilonka; to the Dominick and Covent Garden. If ever I do marry it *must* be a Londoner!"

And she did not know, as the *Queen of the Atlantic* moved steadily out into Southampton Water, that when she did return she was to leave a little of her heart in America.

# 4

# The Disappearing Dancer

**B**efore lunch Drina had explored at least part of the ship, helped by the plan of the accommodation that her grandfather had given her. There were vast halls, with shops and showcases and even a bank, an enormous main lounge, smoking-rooms, writing-rooms, a cinema and a library. There was an immensely long covered deck on either side of the ship and a few people were already lying in the deckchairs on the port side, which would get the sun during the journey.

To Drina it seemed stuffy and very dull and she climbed the steps to the Boat Deck again, and then up more steps to the Games Deck. There was no one at all up there and she stood in a sheltered corner, lost in dreams.

But a glance at her watch told her that it was almost one o'clock, and she was very hungry. She dashed down the first lot of steps, straight into the arms of a tall fair-haired young man of about seventeen or eighteen. He staggered, then seized her in a firm grip, setting her on her feet.

"I guess I wouldn't dash about like that," he said

kindly. "Might be dangerous. Is there a bear up there?"

Drina stared up at him, at once struck by his extreme good looks and by his pleasant American voice. He had only a slight accent and his voice was low and warm. She was also struck painfully by the fact that he thought she was a child, not surprising when her hair was windblown and she had been rushing about like a lunatic.

"I – I remembered that it was lunchtime."

"So it is," he said cheerfully. "But I guess I'll just have a look at the Games Deck." He gave her a funny little bow and went on up the steps.

Drina descended to the Promenade Deck and then to the Main Deck. The staircases were wide, branching and shallow and normally she would have run down them. But she had had one 'accident' and was now conscious of the fact that she was nearly fifteen and not a child. Really, it was getting serious. Young Igor Dominick had taken her for a child when they first met earlier in the year, and now this good-looking young man had done the same. To her astonishment her heart beat faster at the thought of him and there was satisfaction in the knowledge that she would surely see him again.

In their stateroom on A Deck Mr and Mrs Chester were waiting somewhat impatiently.

"I told you to be back here well before one, Drina," Mrs Chester said. "Your grandfather has arranged for a table, but – "

"No harm done," said Mr Chester, as they made their way down to B Deck, where the restaurant was. "What do you think of the ship?"

"Oh, splendid! But so – so vast. It will take days to see it all."

"It's really far too big for comfort," he said, for he was a quiet man and not fond of ostentation.

The restaurant was as enormous as the other rooms and Drina followed her grandparents rather shyly between the flower-decked tables to a table for three against one of the far walls. She had combed her hair and washed her hands, but she wished heartily that she had made time to change her dress.

Faced with an enormous menu that seemed to offer everything under the sun, she looked across at her grandfather and he made some suggestions. People were streaming in, but Drina could only see a section of the restaurant because there was a pillar in the way and so many waiters darting about. However, she did have the satisfaction of seeing the fair-haired young man walking past with a handsome older man and a pretty, grey-haired lady.

"Do you know someone, Drina?" asked her grandmother, noticing her intent gaze, and she blushed.

"No – o, Granny. But I saw that young man on deck."

"A nice-looking boy," said Mrs Chester approvingly. "And his parents – if they *are* his parents – look very pleasant."

"Shall we – get to know anyone?"

"Oh, bound to," said her grandfather cheerfully. "Though there's quite a long passenger list."

"Are there any actresses or film stars? Or dancers, of course. Jan said that he thought Catherine Colby and Peter Bernoise might be on board."

"No actresses or film stars, but you're right about Mr and Mrs Peter Bernoise – and Miss Penelope Bernoise."

"Their little girl! Oh, I wonder if I shall see her? Isn't it wonderful luck that they should be travelling on the *Queen of the Atlantic*? Though," added Drina humbly, "I don't suppose I shall speak to them, even though Catherine Colby did take Rose and me out to lunch once during the *Casse Noisette* rehearsals."

After lunch Drina saw her grandparents settled into chairs on the Promenade Deck, refusing one for herself.

"No, thank you, Granny. I'd feel like a patient in hospital. It's exactly like a ward."

Mrs Chester looked at her doubtfully.

"You do say the most extraordinary things, but I know how restless you are. Just take care, that's all."

"I wonder if the swimming-pool's open yet?"

"I should leave it till tomorrow. You must still have plenty to see and we shall be lying off Cherbourg late this afternoon. We take a lot more passengers on board there."

Drina wandered away, peeped into the nursery, and then chose a couple of books from the well-stocked shelves in the library. The librarian told her that postcards put in the box before Cherbourg would be posted that night and she sat down to write several cards: to Jenny, to Rose, Ilonka and Miss Whiteway. To Rose she wrote:

*This is a picture of the ship. She's wonderful, but so huge. I haven't seen a quarter of her yet. Oh, Rose, I'm glad now that I've come. I've stopped feeling guilty and I know it's going to be marvellous. I wish you were here, too.*

Much later she was wandering down one of the long corridors on A Deck. The lights were so placed that the passage seemed to go on forever, like somewhere in a dream. She was walking slowly, but suddenly stopped altogether, staring in surprise, for it seemed more like a dream than ever. Some way ahead there was a small figure in a yellow dress and the girl had just done some dancing steps that ended in an arabesque. It was rather a wobbly arabesque, as the ship chose that moment to give a decided lurch, but perfectly recognisable as such.

Another dancer on board! How extraordinary!

The girl had glanced over her shoulder and was going on again, away down the seemingly endless corridor. Drina called: "Hey! Do wait a minute!" and began to run.

The other girl stopped and waited for her, though she looked as if she was about to run away. She seemed about thirteen or fourteen and had dark red hair in a gleaming ponytail. Her face looked white and pinched, though Drina wondered briefly if perhaps it was the lights that made her look so pale.

"I saw you dance and I'm a dancer, too. I'm Drina Adams. What's your name?"

"Yolande Mason."

"And you do learn ballet?"

"I – Yes," said the stranger. Her voice was light and a little breathless, as though she were very anxious or shy. "I went to the Lingeraux School."

"In Bloomsbury Square? I know. I'm at the Dominick, but – " And then Drina heard her grandmother's voice behind her and spun round to see Mrs Chester standing on the corner near the broad hallway where the stairs and the lifts were.

"Drina!"

"I'll come back, Yolande," she said hastily and ran towards her grandmother. Mrs Chester looked tired and said that she was going to lie down for an hour.

"I've had a lot to do lately and I'm tired. Besides, the Channel is decidedly choppy and I haven't got my sea-legs yet. I do wish you wouldn't run."

"No, Granny. I'm trying not to." But how easy it was to forget.

"It isn't safe, even though down here it's difficult to realise that we're at sea. If you want any tea you can get it anywhere. Just sit in the main lounge or one of the garden lounges."

"Yes, Granny." Drina conscientiously saw her grandmother to her cabin and waited until she was settled comfortably. Then she hurried back to find the other dancer. But the corridor was quite empty, except for a couple of stewardesses talking together some distance away.

Intrigued, and impatient to learn more about the girl who said, "I *went* to the Lingeraux School" and not "I go," Drina looked into every one of the public rooms, feeling small and conspicuous as she crossed the vast main lounge, where a few people were listening to light orchestral music. A cheerful tune followed her as she looked into the writing-room, the smoking-rooms and the two garden lounges.

She went along the deserted side of the covered deck, up on to the Boat Deck, where the wind was chilly and the rows of white lifeboats were raised against a sky that was startlingly blue; up on to the Games Deck; down again on to a little sheltered open deck. Finally, without finding Yolande, she marched along the port side of the Promenade Deck to where her grandfather was reading.

"How goes it, Drina?" he asked.

"It's like three or four big hotels, with the concourse at Euston Station thrown in," Drina remarked, sinking down on to her grandmother's empty chair. "I've been looking for someone. There was a girl – " And she told him the story of the odd little encounter.

"Look in the passenger list," Mr Chester said. "Here it is. If you've got her name right you can ask at the Purser's Bureau. They'll tell you her cabin number."

But there was no Yolande Mason on the passenger list that he handed to her, and no name remotely like it. Drina frowned, very puzzled.

"I didn't *imagine* her. She was pale and looked nervy,

somehow. She was wearing a yellow dress and she *spoke* to me."

"Perhaps she joined the ship at the last moment. I should go and ask."

But at the Bureau they could tell her nothing about a girl called Yolande Mason, and Drina retreated more puzzled than ever, but determined to find the other dancer.

By six o'clock on a rather blowy evening the *Queen of the Atlantic* was lying off Cherbourg and a tender was bringing passengers and luggage out to the ship. Drina, wearing a belted raincoat, stood on deck to watch the excitement and to stare at France, though there was not much to see but unattractive buildings and distant fields. By then she was in a dazed state, for it was all so new and she scarcely felt like Drina Adams at all.

At half-past seven, when she and her grandparents went down to the restaurant, the passengers were still coming on board through an opening on B Deck nearby. Everywhere was littered with mountains of cases and boxes and the new arrivals looked chilly, wind-blown and bewildered. There were a number of French children and a party of nuns also talking French. A couple of stewards were sending people in different directions.

"Tourist Class aft," Drina heard him say, and the words seemed to solve her problem. Of course! How silly she had been not to think of it. If Yolande Mason wasn't to be found amongst the first-class passengers, then she must be travelling Tourist. She said as much to her grandfather, who nodded.

"You're probably right. Where did you meet her?"

"On A Deck. Quite a long way down from our cabins. Let me see – aft."

"She may have come through from the Tourist Class part, then. People do wander about, especially on the first day."

"Could I go and look for her?"

"Of course, but you'd better wait till morning, though, Drina."

Dinner was a very splendid meal and Drina enjoyed it. It was fun to watch the people and to savour the air of warmth and luxury, though, as it was the first night, few people had dressed up. Drina herself wore her turquoise blue dress and the necklace and ear-rings that her Italian grandmother had given her when she was in Milan. She had brushed her hair till it shone and given her face a careful dusting of powder. She would have liked to add lipstick, only Mrs Chester heartily disapproved of make-up for girls her age. They had an argument about it only the last time that Drina went to the theatre – on one of the nights when she had been a spectator instead of a performer in Edinburgh.

"You are far too young," Mrs Chester had said.

But Drina, already an expert with make-up because of her stage experience, thought that lipstick made her look far prettier and certainly much less childish. But she had won over the evening shoes with heels and she was wearing them now.

Afterwards the Chesters and Drina sat in the main lounge and Mr Chester said suddenly, "There are the people you liked the look of, Drina! The name's Rossiter. I got talking to Mr Rossiter this afternoon. I'll introduce you to them. They're coming over."

Drina's heart leaped as she found the fair-haired young man approaching with his parents. She scarcely heard the introductions except to note, with pleasure, that the young man was called Grant. Grant Rossiter! Yes, it sounded just right. He was smiling at her and

saying that they had met before on deck. He could see her pretty ear-rings. Surely, surely, he wouldn't still think her a child?

She felt tongue-tied and was annoyed with herself, but the others did not seem to have noticed. The Rossiters were explaining that they had been for a holiday to Europe and that Grant was starting work in his father's office on Fifth Avenue at the beginning of October. They had wanted him to go to a University, but he wasn't all that keen on studying. Grant added that music and climbing were his great interests and he had been able to satisfy both while in Britain. Concerts in London and then he had joined a climbing party in North Wales.

Drina, who had once stayed in Snowdonia for six weeks, and who had gleaned from Jenny's brother Philip a lot of information about the various famous climbs, opened her mouth to say something, but the subject was changed. The elder Rossiters were talking about New York hotels and Grant's whole attention seemed to be given to a flaxen-haired girl in a sea-green dress who had just come in. She had a rather vacant face, doll-like and without expression, but the figure of a model. Drina hated her fiercely and couldn't wholly understand herself. She seemed to be filled with unfamiliar emotions; it was all very curious and not entirely pleasant.

She did manage to make a few remarks when Mrs Rossiter said that she thought there was a European ballet company billed to appear at the Metropolitan Opera House the following week.

"Oh, what luck! Which company is it? What are they doing?"

"She thinks of nothing but ballet," said Mrs Chester.

"I think it's a French company," Mrs Rossiter offered

after a moment. "Yes, I guess it's one from Paris. I think they're dancing *Giselle*, for one."

"Oh, I wonder if we can still get seats!"

"I'll try," Mr Chester said. "It's a huge place, after all."

Soon after that Grant excused himself and wandered away and Mrs Chester said firmly to Drina that she had better go to bed, as it had been a long day.

"And remember to put your watch back an hour," she said, as Drina rose obediently. "I'll come and see you presently."

It was only when she was sitting at the dressing-table in her cabin, staring at her flushed face in the looking-glass, that Drina realised the astonishing truth. She had fallen in love. It had happened the moment she saw Grant, the thing that people talked about, that books and plays and ballets were nearly always based on, but that she had not expected to happen to her for years and years, if ever. She had thought dancing her whole life and that there would be no room for love. And then casually, between one moment and the next, she had fallen in love with a tall, fair-haired soft-voiced New Yorker.

"And there are only five days," she thought, as she undressed, washed and climbed into bed. "Five days to see him and listen to him."

When Mrs Chester came she pretended to be almost asleep, and her grandmother turned out the light and went quietly away again.

But Drina lay for a long time, conscious of the throbbing of the distant engines, her cheeks hot and her heart beating faster than usual.

It seemed so long since that morning when she stood on deck at the moment of departure. Already it seemed natural to be on the *Queen of the Atlantic* and she had a dim feeling that the voyage was going to be a kind of strange mixture of happiness and pain.

When she slept at last she had one of her "ballet dreams". She was dancing in *Giselle* – she was Giselle and Grant Rossiter was Albrecht. She could see the two familiar little houses on either side of the stage and hear the music that she knew so well. Only things were not going right: Albrecht was dancing with the Queen of the Wilis, which was wrong in itself, as the Queen of the Wilis didn't appear until the second act. What was worse still was that the Queen wore sea-green instead of white and was the girl Grant had seemed to admire in the lounge.

Drina started to protest and the music stopped. The stage disappeared and she was dancing on and on along an endless shining corridor, while her grandmother's voice implored her stop. But she couldn't stop. She danced on and through some open doors and into the dark, cold sea.

She awoke thankfully to see by the illuminated dial of her watch that it was three o'clock, and the ship was heading steadily towards America.

# 5

# Yolande

When Drina woke again it was still dark, naturally, as her cabin had no porthole, but the time was half-past seven. She turned on all the lights and saw that several things had been pushed under the door. The ship's newspaper *The Ocean Times*, the programme for the day and a single printed sheet that turned out to be a competition about naming the authors of famous books.

Drina put them all aside for later, after a glance at the programme told her the swimming-pool opened at seven. They had agreed to have breakfast at nine, so there was plenty of time for a swim.

After the night's sleep her strange feelings of the evening before had receded and she almost believed that she had imagined the whole thing. But the first person she saw as she stood on the edge of the pool in her new red swimsuit was Grant Rossiter. There were only two or three people in the water and he was swimming rapidly towards her, his fair hair darkened and his face dripping wet.

"Hi, Drina! Good morning! Coming in?"

Drina's heart leapt up and then settled into place again. She said as calmly as she could. "Of course. Is it cold?"

"Not bad at all. I guess you'll survive," he said grinning, and she dived in neatly, glad that she swam quite well. For ten minutes they raced up and down the pool and, though Grant won every time, he congratulated her on the style and speed of her swimming. Drina was happy until she felt his attention wander and saw that the flaxen-haired girl, now in a sea-green bikini instead of a dress, was testing the water with her toe.

She plunged in, not nearly so neatly as Drina, and either by accident or design came up practically nose to nose with Grant. They both laughed and in no time at all Grant was giving her a diving lesson. Drina, astonished at the sharp pain somewhere in her chest, swam a little more and then decided that the water *was* cold and she would go and have a hot saltwater bath to restore her circulation.

She was very quiet at breakfast and her grandmother was rather concerned.

"Are you sure you feel all right? You can't be feeling seasick, surely? The ship's very steady now."

"I'm quite all right, thank you, Granny." Drina knew that on no account must her grandmother guess at the new emotions that filled her. If she objected to a little lipstick she would certainly think Drina too young to be in love. In any case it was unthinkable that anyone should guess; pride alone would make her keep it entirely to herself.

After breakfast she went off to look for Yolande Mason, walking along the corridor on A Deck until, in the end, she came to a low wooden gate that turned out to be unlocked. It had seemed impossible to her that there should be any more space on the ship, but there was a whole other world – a large lounge, smoking-rooms, another library, a shop, a nursery. They were all smaller than the ones she knew, but the lounge was very pleasant and far more homely than the enormous first-class one.

Fascinated, she almost forgot about Yolande, and before she had made any enquiries she actually met the girl with the ponytail. Yolande was coming up from the swimming-pool, her hair damp and her swimsuit in her hand.

They stared at each other and then Drina cried:

"Oh, *there* you are! I'm sorry you didn't wait yesterday. I do so want to hear about your dancing. Can we go to your cabin and talk?"

"Yes. Then I can dry my hair," Yolande agreed and she led the way up two flights of stairs and along a passage that was narrower and very much hotter than the shining one where they had first met. But her cabin was an outside one and, though there was an extra bunk, she seemed to have it to herself.

"Someone moved out," Yolande explained, seeing Drina's curious glance. "I was really pleased. She met someone she knew and there was room in the other cabin. I needed – I needed dreadfully to be alone." She offered Drina the armchair and sank down on the bed with a dry towel in her hand. The bright morning light fell through the porthole on to her face and Drina saw that the strange girl did indeed look very pale, and there was a nervous little twitch to one eyebrow.

"But you don't mind talking to me, do you?"

"No, I – I'd like to. I'd like to hear about the Dominick. I've seen it often, of course, painted blue in Red Lion Square. And I've seen the company dance. Someone said that Catherine Colby is actually on board."

"Well, she's on the passenger list. She and her husband, Peter Bernoise – he's the principal male dancer, of course – and their little daughter Penelope. But I haven't seen them yet. The ship's so huge and there are a lot of passengers."

"And are you going to live in America?" Yolande rubbed her hair as she spoke.

"Good gracious no! Grandfather's going to a Conference in New York and Granny and I are going along, too. I didn't think at first that I ought to miss my dancing, but Miss Volonaise said it would be all right."

"Did you say you were Drina Adams? It sounds sort of familiar, and I thought at once that I knew you. Did you have your picture in one of the London papers a few months ago, and then the same one on the cover of a ballet magazine?"

"Yes. Dancing by a fountain on Isola Bella. Fancy your remembering!"

Yolande looked a good deal more animated and when she smiled she was very pretty.

"I thought it was a lovely picture. I cut it out. And then there was something in *Ballet Today* about your being picked to dance Little Clara in *Casse Noisette* at the Edinburgh Festival."

"Yes. That's why everyone said I could come to America; because I'd worked in the holidays."

"I never thought *I'd* meet anyone famous! Not to talk to her like a friend. But the magazine said you were nearly fifteen and you look younger than me."

"I'll be fifteen in a few weeks' time. I wish I didn't look so young," Drina said ruefully. "And I'm not a bit famous. How old are you?"

"Fourteen in November. And," the rather sad green-grey eyes clouded, "I *am* going to live in America."

Drina stared at her in astonishment, but at least it explained why she had spoken of the Lingeraux School in the past tense.

"Are you all alone?"

"Yes, sort of in charge of the stewardess. You see," and it came out with a rush, "I'm an orphan and I lived with an aunt in London. Well, she was French, really, but she'd lived in London for twenty years. She was my only relation in Britain. Mother was French and Father was American, but I feel nothing but British and – and when my aunt died I thought I should die, too. It was all so dreadful and there was only Mrs Penny, Auntie's friend, and Madame at the Lingeraux. Then Aunt Grace wrote from New York and said that of course I must go and live with her, but I still wanted to die. I don't know her, and America is a foreign country, isn't it? But there wasn't anything else to do. People our age are so helpless."

"I know," agreed Drina, who had often, with some resentment, thought the same thing. "But you may like New York and I expect your aunt is nice. Though it's awful having to change countries, and if *I* had to leave the Dominick I'd want to die, too."

"I liked the Lingeraux," said Yolande, "*and* Madame. But I think they were beginning to think I'd never make a dancer."

"Oh, dear! Aren't you good, then?"

"Yes, in a way," Yolande said slowly, plucking nervously at the towel which now lay across her knee. "I've got good technique for my age and – oh, you'd never understand! You danced in Edinburgh in front of all those critical people. I haven't got any confidence and it's got worse and worse. I – I go to pieces when I have to dance in front of people, though I *love* it. I can't really bear to give it up. That was why I danced yesterday, when you saw me. Just to know that it was still there. Still part of me. I wasn't always afraid of people, but just lately, even before Auntie died, I made a mess of things. We had a show at the Lingeraux Theatre and I had quite a big part, but somehow – I couldn't go on. I just *couldn't* face all those people! And everyone was angry, and – puzzled. And I felt so ashamed.''

Drina stared at her, appalled.

''But why? People are often nervous, of course. I am myself. But once I get on the stage – ''

''I don't know. I couldn't explain, and I can't now. I hadn't been very well. And now I feel I'll never be able to try again. I – I know I'm a coward, but – ''

''But of course you'll have to try again. It's bound to pass. It's just nerves. Dancers are always a bit temperamental and that's one of the things that annoy Granny.''

''I thought when I heard that I was leaving the Lingeraux that that would be the end of it,'' Yolande said. ''One side of me was almost glad, and the other side minded dreadfully. Then Aunt Grace wrote to say that she wouldn't make any definite plans about a new school until I arrived and had had a good rest, but she was sure I'd want to keep on my dancing. There's a ballet school on Madison Avenue – the Madison-Maperley School of Dance – and I'm going there for classes straight away.''

''Oh!'' Immediately Drina's thoughts flashed ahead. Even though she would only be in New York such a short time it might be possible to attend a few classes. It would be interesting and probably stimulating to have a new teacher and the staff at the Dominick would not mind. ''I wonder if I could go, too? Just a few times. I'd love it!''

Yolande's quick, attractive smile flashed out again and she cried eagerly, ''Oh, *would* you? It would make such a difference to go with someone I know.''

"I'd have to ask Granny and she's sure not to be very keen, but she doesn't try to oppose me now about dancing."

They talked for some time and Drina learned that Yolande was going to live in Greenwich Village.

"In somewhere called MacDougal Alley. Aunt Grace said in one of her letters that she's sure I'll like it. It's a little quiet street, with some little old houses, just near Washington Square. You could come to tea, perhaps."

"I'd love to see Greenwich Village. It's the art part, isn't it, like Montmartre in Paris? I can't really believe," Drina confessed, "that on Tuesday morning we'll sail into New York harbour."

When she left Yolande, having promised to see her again that afternoon to play deck tennis, Drina's mind was very busy. She liked and was sorry for her new friend, for she understood very well the misery through which Yolande must have gone. It was bad enough to lose her aunt and to be going to a strange country all alone, but far worse to have lost her nerve over dancing in front of an audience. That might well be a tragedy, especially if Yolande really showed promise, and she had seen too many tragedies at the Dominick to take anyone's dancing problems lightly.

Late that afternoon Drina sat in the writing-room, writing to Rose. The letter wouldn't be posted until they reached New York, of course, but it would go by air in only a couple of days. And she needed to confide her thoughts and new experiences to someone. Jenny – it should have been Jenny. But Jenny seemed to have gone further away than Drina would have believed possible, and, in any case, it seemed to her unfair to describe her new and exciting experiences when Jenny was having such difficulties.

*Dear Rose,* she wrote in her neat, slightly sloping hand,

*Here I am on the* Queen of the Atlantic *and most of the time I don't feel like myself at all. It is all so new and the ship is so immense. You can walk and walk and walk. Wonder of wonders! Catherine Colby and Peter Bernoise are on board. I didn't see them until nearly teatime today and then I came face to face with Catherine Colby in the hall on the Promenade Deck. I just smiled and was going to pass, but she stopped and said, "Fancy seeing you on the* Queen of the Atlantic, *Drina! Come and have tea with us." You know how nice she was when we were rehearsing for* Casse Noisette, *but I never expected her to bother with me here.*

*Anyway, I had tea with her in the main lounge, and Peter Bernoise and their little girl Penelope were there, too. Penelope is really lovely, just as fair as her mother and with a sweet little piping voice. C.C. says they don't really want Penelope to be a dancer, but she is very musical already and is always trying to dance. I didn't think that she (C.C.) looked very well and she told me that she hasn't been too good since Edinburgh. They are going to America on holiday to visit some relatives, and the season at the Dominick will start without them, with Renée Randall dancing most of the ballerina roles.*

*I have met a very nice girl called Yolande Mason, who used to be at the Lingeraux, but now she is going to live in New York. She is going to classes at a dancing school on Madison Avenue, and I think I may try to go there as well a few times. It would be fun to dance in New York and would mean that I shouldn't be so much out of practice.*

*A lot of people on board are American and there are some nice people called Rossiter. They have a son, about eighteen, called Grant, very handsome with fair hair and a nice soft, slightly drawly voice. He thought I was a child, which hurt rather, but now I don't think he quite thinks that. I swam with him this morning and after lunch I met him on deck. He seems to like a girl called Peggy Carling; she's pretty and has a beautiful figure, but is a bit stupid, I think. She's just starting as a model, so Mrs Rossiter said, and she got the chance to work in N.Y. for a short time, though she's only seventeen. However, she looks far older.* This was as far as Drina could go, even to Rose, where her feelings for Grant were concerned.

*There is to be a Fancy Headdress Competition on Saturday evening, and a concert on the last night, and there are really plenty of things to do, like playing table tennis and deck tennis and swimming.*

*Oh, Rose, I wish you were here! It was such fun in Edinburgh. And if you were here it would somehow help to make it feel more real. I never feel quite that I'm me, and I expect it will be just the same in New York.*

*New York! Think of it. Think of seeing Fifth Avenue, and standing on top of a skyscraper, and actually sitting in the Metropolitan Opera House. It looks very easy to get about. The streets are nearly all numbered in order. The ones that run north and south are called Avenues and numbered from east to west – First Avenue, Second, up to Twelfth by the docks where we get in. Oh, and Broadway, of course, going on for miles and not straight like the others. I long to see the Great White Way with all the theatres. Then the cross-town streets start near the bottom and work up.*

*What a long letter and it won't be posted till Tuesday morning in New York.*

*Lots of love*

*from*

*Drina*

*Stop press!*

*The Assistant Purser has asked me if I will dance at the concert on Monday evening. There is an orchestra on board, and he said they could play most things! I said I couldn't possibly dance with Catherine Colby and Peter Bernoise on board but the A.P. said it was Miss Colby who suggested it. Granny* doesn't seem keen, but I suppose I shall have to do it. I've got a new dance running through my mind, to that tune we rather like, Twentieth Century Serenade. It always seemed to me that it should have movement to it. So here's to Drina Adams, the great choreographer – perhaps!

# 6

# Drina Turns Choreographer

That evening Drina stayed up late, as her grandmother thought that she was getting plenty of sleep now they were putting the clocks back an hour each night. Wearing the scarlet dress bought in Milan, she watched the horse-racing in the lounge and then wandered into the ballroom, where a few couples were dancing. Catherine Colby and Peter Bernoise were there, though not dancing, but Drina scarcely gave them a glance because she immediately saw Grant Rossiter dancing with Peggy Carling.

She stood near the door, feeling very young and small, and with a most unfamiliar ache in her heart. At that moment she would have given almost anything to be a couple of years older and as "slinky" and glamorous as Grant's partner. Nearly fifteen was a wretched age to be, especially when you looked little more than twelve.

For the next dance Peggy was asked to dance by an older man, and Grant looked round, then began to walk towards Drina. Her heart gave a quite sickening leap of mingled panic and pleasure. He was going to ask her to dance ... No, he was just making for the door.

But Grant did come up, smiling.

"Why don't we dance, Drina? Or don't you count ballroom dancing? I didn't know you were a professional until your grandmother told my mother."

"I'd love to dance," Drina said breathlessly. "And – and I'm not really a pro. yet. That is, I have a licence and – "

"You've had parts in West End plays and danced at the Edinburgh Festival. *And* danced in Italy with the Dominick."

"Only once. And – and it was be – because the *corps de ballet* ate lobster and several of them were ill."

He laughed. Already they were moving round the floor and Drina was thankful that she had bothered to learn ballroom dancing, though she had never been very keen on it. But now it was not dull at all. It was one of the nicest things that had ever happened to her. Grant danced well, and he was so tall that her nose was well below the knot of his tie.

"Poor members of the *corps de ballet*! But you must be good to have been asked. Look! I see Catherine Colby over there with her husband. *Could* you introduce me?"

A little of the magic promptly went. He had only asked her because of that, then. But she answered:

"Of course. She's very nice."

"She's a wonderful dancer, but I heard a rumour that she was going to retire."

"It can't be true!" Drina said, quite sharply, forgetting to be shy. "Don't say anything to her. I'm sure it can't be true. It would be dreadful!"

"Sure I won't," he agreed cheerfully. "It *would* be dreadful. I guess the world would lose one of its greatest dancers."

When the dance ended Drina led him towards Peter

Bernoise and Catherine Colby and, trying to sound confident and grown up, introduced him to them. They were both natural and charming people and the young American – and Drina – were soon sitting with them. Drina was content merely to sit and listen. How very odd it was to be so happy just watching someone and listening to them talk. Jenny, surely, would have thought her thoroughly sentimental, and Drina wondered if perhaps she would have been right. But, sentimental or not, that was how it was. And only a few more days remained. Once they docked, New York would swallow Grant up. It was a very depressing thought.

In the night Drina awoke and found that, while she slept, in the curious way in which these things sometimes happen, her dance had come much clearer in her mind. But it needed two dancers to be exactly what she wanted and she had the sudden brilliant idea of including Yolande. It was high time that Yolande gained confidence again. Once she had faced the shipboard audience she would probably never be scared again.

After breakfast Drina went to the Assistant Purser and put forward her suggestion. He nodded.

"Yes, if you're sure the other girl dances well enough."

"I feel in my bones that she's good," said Drina, and he laughed and turned away.

Drina made her way down the long corridor, through the gate, down the stairs and along passages to Yolande's cabin. Yolande was there, washing tights, and she looked rather appalled when she heard the suggestion.

"It's very nice of you, Drina, but I couldn't possibly. I told you – "

"I know you did. But I'm sure being afraid was only a passing thing and I'd love you to dance."

"But I've got nothing suitable to wear. My tutus are in my trunk in the hold; even my practice costume is. I've got some shoes, but – "

"Don't worry. I don't think we can do much about costumes. We shall have to wear one of our ordinary dresses. I thought I'd wear my white one without the belt. It's very soft and short and full. If you had one that would go with it – "

Fired by her enthusiasm, Yolande began to spread dresses on the bed. She had quite a number. Drina pounced on a soft pale green one and held it up.

"This would do brilliantly! It's very like mine in style and such a pretty colour. Oh, Yolande, do say you'll do it! It will ruin everything if you won't, and I was awake for ages last night planning things."

"But where could we practise?"

"It's a bit difficult, but I think Granny and Grandfather's cabin will have to do. There's really quite a lot of floor space and several long mirrors and Granny said we could use it. I got a copy of *Twentieth Century Serenade* from the leader of the orchestra last night and we'll have to hum for the most part. I expect we could have one or two rehearsals with the orchestra before Monday evening. The only thing that really worries me is that time is so short. We'll have to work really hard."

Yolande faced her, the green dress held under her chin.

"How do you know I'm good enough? How do you know I won't let you down? I'll try not to, but – but – oh, no, I'd better not!"

"I'm sure you're good. You say so yourself, and I did see those few steps. It was a very nice arabesque until the movement of the ship made you wobble. And you won't let me down. I'll trust you."

"But you don't know – you don't understand. Something awful comes over me. When I think of all those people – "

"*Don't* think of them, then. Just think of the dance. Come along and we'll try it out. Where are your shoes?"

As they hurried towards the large cabin on A Deck Drina said, "You have to trust *me*, too. I'm making the dance up, the first time I ever seriously have. But I've always wanted to try."

"A choreographer, too!" There was flattering awe in Yolande's voice, but Drina only laughed.

"It's a grand word for a little dance. Do you know *Twentieth Century Serenade*?"

For answer Yolande burst into tuneful whistling and Drina joined in, for she whistled quite well herself. They passed along the long corridor, smiled at by a few lingering stewards and stewardesses, and, reaching the cabin, were soon deeply absorbed.

Drina, at first rather diffidently, hummed, whistled and demonstrated, and then, as her ideas took fire with actual performance, more confidently. She was relieved to see that her instinctive judgment had been sound; Yolande danced well and had a pure technique. She had seemed to find no difficulty whatsoever in following Drina's instructions.

But Drina saw that her first ideas had not always been the right ones. In performance some of the steps and movements did not flow easily into each other; did not fully interpret the picture she had in mind. She altered and augmented and was once more followed effortlessly by Yolande. Using mainly classical steps, but with here and there more modern movements, Drina gradually built up the dance she wanted. The satisfaction was enormous: she was gradually filled

with a glowing feeling of achievement.

After a long time they both flopped down on the beds to rest.

"In a way it's a pity you're not a boy," Drina remarked. "Then it would be a proper *pas de deux*. And yet I think that two girls fulfil my idea better. You do see what I've tried to do, don't you? Of course it's a ballet without a story, but it does mean something. At first the young people are sort of dreamy and unaware, and then suddenly they become sharply aware of being alive and all the rest is them living, being happy and suffering and sort of praising the time they live in. The twentieth century, of course."

"I do see and I think it's brilliant. I think you're really clever. But I wish we had the proper music."

Yolande was quite pink with eagerness and no longer looked so tense and nervous.

"Next time they have a record evening we might ask them if they could play *Twentieth Century Serenade*," said Drina. "They're sure to have it. That would be a help, and one or two of the recordings are splendid, with lovely drums and brasses. Of course we won't get it fully orchestrated on the night."

Soon after that they began to dance again and Drina was struck anew with amazement at the way her ideas had come to life, even to their rather breathless whistling and humming, with frequent consultations of the music to make sure that they had got each part right. It was almost like a miracle, and it filled her with delight. To make dances as well as to interpret other people's ideas – that was something new and very exciting.

That evening before dinner Drina wrote to Ilonka, another letter to be posted when they reached New York. *Oh, Ilonka, it's all splendid. The ship is wonderful and so far, except just in the middle of the Channel on the way to Cherbourg, I'd hardly know we were at sea. You can't even see the sea from most of the rooms and corridors, in fact you have to walk quite a long way to see it, and even further to get a breath of air. The food is simply wonderful; you can have anything and I adore the way that everything is iced. Even the breakfast grapefruit juice comes to the table sitting on a whole bed of ice. Granny isn't keen and says the Americans are far too fond of ice, but I love it all the time. I've had salmon and fresh strawberries, gorgeous gateau and even caviare.*

*There are some nice people, particularly an American family called Rossiter. Grant Rossiter, their son, is really nice and I played table tennis with him this afternoon and beat him twice, too, which seemed to surprise him. He treats me rather as though I'm a child, which annoys me a bit. He has fair hair and a lovely voice, only a bit American. He does say "I guess" occasionally, and "Yeah" instead of yes. Another trick he has is to say "Why don't we – ?" instead of "Shall we?". "Why don't we play table tennis?" I rather like it and I'm sure you'd like him. He seems much more grown up than Igor, and of course he's eighteen.*

*There is a very nice girl called Yolande Mason on board. She is a dancer, too, isn't it a coincidence? She and I are going to dance at the concert on Monday evening, and I have made up a dance to* Twentieth Century Serenade. *It quite surprises me, as it is going so well, though rehearsing it is really difficult. We started in Grandfather's and Granny's cabin, but later on we danced for a bit on the starboard side of the covered Prom. Deck. A few people came past and looked surprised, but on the whole it is very empty.*

*The port side is the sunny one and everyone lies there in deckchairs, with rugs over them. Especially when the steward brings round the morning soup it reminds me of a hospital! Granny gets quite annoyed when I say so. But I always want to laugh. I feel as though I should be bringing fruit and flowers and asking about their operations!*

*I do hope you are enjoying the new term and that everything is going well at "The Golden Zither." Has Terza finished her book yet? I must admit that the Dominick seems very far away, and so do you all. Yolande and I have a lot in common. This afternoon we compared notes and we find that we like and hate a lot of the same things. She hates people who eat in the theatre, particularly chocolates and sweets wrapped in cellophane – terribly rattly stuff; I wonder who invented it? She loves the Solitaire music. She also loves the Rose Adagio, and that glorious bit in Sylvia near the beginning, when Sylvia first appears to that wonderful music, with the strange drum notes. You know how I was haunted by those drums, the first time I saw the ballet at Covent Garden, and had to beg Grandfather to buy me a record?*

*Yolande and I have talked and talked about ballet and I've begged Grandfather to get an extra ticket for the Metropolitan if there are any seats left by the time we get there. Mrs Rossiter says it is a French ballet company and they are doing Giselle.*

*Do please write to N.Y. New York! It seems more and more fantastic that we'll be there early on Tuesday morning. I feel as though we could sail on forever, never arriving anywhere.*

*A quarter to seven. I must go and change. I've worn my blue dress and my scarlet one, and I really want to keep my white one for the concert. The scarlet one is really the only fairly grown up dress that I have. Granny has promised to take me to Saks Fifth Avenue, the poshest shop in New York, I think, and buy me two new ones. I'd like a yellow one and an emerald green one, so here's hoping!*

*Love from,*
*Drina*

# 7

# Ship's Concert

Sunday passed and Drina felt more and more absorbed into the life of the ship. More and more, too, she treasured every hour that they were at sea, for on Tuesday Grant Rossiter would disappear into the great unknown city. At times she was humbly content just to see him; striding along the deck, his hair ruffled by the wind, playing deck tennis, entering the restaurant in the evening. But unfortunately that state of contentment never lasted long and she felt more knife-thrusts of jealousy and longing than she had ever before experienced.

Her feelings continued to disconcert and rather appal her and she fought fiercely with herself, determined that, for no reason, would any of it show on her face. How dreadful if her grandmother guessed! How equally dreadful if Grant himself guessed. She told herself that it must all be part of growing up, but it was difficult not to be angry with fate because she had fallen in love with someone so completely unattainable and unseeable, once the voyage was over. If it had been someone at the Dominick she would at least have known where he was at most hours of the day and would not have this almost desperate awareness of the precious, passing days.

But there were happy hours, too, when Grant came up to her in his casual, friendly way. "Why don't we go and play table tennis? I guess I'll beat you this time." "Why don't we have another swim?" "Why don't we dance this?" Afterwards he would go off equally casually and she might see him talking to Peggy Carling. Peggy looked stunning in everything, from a swimsuit to tightly cut jeans and a high-necked sweater, but she did not do much except dancing and an occasional swim. Besides, and this was a comfort to Drina in a way, she had plenty of other admirers and often held court in a sheltered corner of the deck or in one of the main rooms.

"If she were my daughter," Mrs Chester said once, disapprovingly, "I wouldn't let her come to America with those four other girls. Of course that Mrs Jenkins is supposed to be in charge of them, but she seems to spend most of her time reading on the covered deck or sitting in the bar."

"She's very pretty," said Drina. "Peggy, I mean."

"Pretty! She's a little madam and barely seventeen. I don't know what her mother can be thinking of." Mrs Chester had somewhat rigid views and liked girls to be quiet and what she thought of as "properly behaved".

"Granny, what were you like when you were fifteen or sixteen?"

Mrs Chester put down her book, removed her spectacles and looked at Drina in some astonishment.

"Like? I hope I knew how to behave. I didn't have much fun, though, as I've often told you. I had an invalid mother."

"But how did you *feel*?" It seemed suddenly very important to know.

Mrs Chester looked back down a busy and mainly happy life, though not without its tragedies – her mother's early death and then her only daughter's death on that ill-fated flight to America.

"Feel? I don't know. Some people say they remember exactly what it was like to be young. I can't say I can, though. I only remember the things that stand out. Mother's funeral, and my first dance, and the first time I fell in love."

"The first time? Wasn't it Grandfather, then?"

Mrs Chester actually laughed.

"Good gracious no! I was twenty-two when I first met your grandfather. The first one was the boy next door. I suppose I was about fourteen and he was a couple of years older. He was called Percy and he had dreadful spots, but I only really noticed them when I'd fallen out of love again."

"*Did* you fall out of love, then?"

"Well, naturally. What would you expect at fourteen? Though one does hear of young people who grow up together and later marry. After that I think it was Rudolph – he was the son of some friends of my mother. Now he was very good-looking and I don't say it mightn't have lasted, but he was a very unsettled young man and eventually he went out to Canada and soon married there. I cried when Rudolph went away," Mrs Chester went on, sounding rather astonished. "And I wasn't really one for crying about anything. After that there wasn't anyone really special until I met your grandfather and that was the end of it – or the beginning, of course."

Drina was very impressed by all this as well as surprised. It had never occurred to her that her controlled and unemotional grandmother had had such wayward feelings. But the new knowledge didn't make her any more anxious to have her own secret known, and she went to look for Yolande in a very thoughtful frame of mind, which only changed when they were deep in their rehearsal.

She liked Yolande more and more and was delighted with her dancing and the intelligent way that Yolande was able to interpret her suggestions. In spite of the many difficulties, *Twentieth Century Serenade* was a very definite reality, and when they managed a rehearsal with the orchestra in the almost deserted ballroom just before lunch on the Monday she was amazed and delighted by the completeness of her creation. In the ballroom there was a small but well-equipped stage. It was really too small for their purpose and the main difficulty was to confine their movements to its proportions.

Yolande made no protest about dancing in front of the orchestra, and in fact Drina had almost forgotten about her friend's past troubles.

"What shall we do if we get an encore?" Drina asked, as they rested and chatted to the leader of the orchestra. "We haven't anything else."

In the end it was decided that they should repeat the last part of the ballet, the two little solo dances and the coda.

So everything seemed settled and Drina went off in high spirits to tidy her hair before lunch. It was nice to know that probably she would not disgrace herself, especially as Grant would be there. Well, she supposed – even passionately hoped – that he would be there. He knew that she was dancing – oh, *surely* he would come? For the first time in her life, and she was rather ashamed about it, she was looking forward to dancing in front of just one special person.

Monday! The last day. That morning she had woken up early and had lain thinking about it. She felt that she simply could not see beyond it, for not only would it mean her last meeting with Grant (though surely she might have a glimpse of him on Tuesday morning?), but it would bring the plunge into the unknown city very near.

But as the day passed much as the others had done, she found it almost impossible to believe that there would not be other days at sea. New York seemed an unlikely dream, not a reality of concrete and steel and glass only a few hours away across the sea. And yet she had packed her cases for removal by the steward that evening, and only her small overnight case remained open and still half-empty.

Before dinner they managed another short rehearsal and by then Yolande looked very pale and not too happy. But she danced as well as before and Drina's mind was so occupied that she scarcely noticed. She was not really very nervous herself, though she did hope fervently that everything would go off well. After all, they had only been rehearsing since Saturday and it *was* a very short time, even for such a simple ballet.

At dinner Mrs Chester looked at her anxiously when she refused any pudding.

"What's the matter? Not worried, are you? I really do wish that they hadn't asked you to dance. You don't seem able to escape it for a moment."

"She enjoys it," said Mr Chester.

"I'm all right, Granny, honestly. Only I'll never be able to dance a step if I eat any more."

"The concert doesn't start until half-past nine, and you're not on very early. Fifth, is it?"

"Yes, fifth." But Drina escaped as soon as she could and went for a walk along the chilly and totally deserted Promenade Deck. Through the windows she could just see the black water swishing past. It would be strange not to be on the sea, not hearing the throb of the

engines and feeling the slight movement of the ship.
And Grant would be gone. Her heart gave a sort of
wrench at the very thought.

At nine o'clock she was in her cabin, tying back her
hair with a ribbon and making sure that her shoes were
all right. Most of her luggage had gone now, because of
the early disembarkation, and the fact made her feel
oddly desolate. The rather stuffy cabin had become her
"home".

Yolande had said that she would be at Drina's cabin
by a quarter-past nine, so that they could be in their
places to see the beginning of the concert. But by
twenty-past nine she hadn't come and uneasiness
suddenly boiled up in Drina. Now she remembered
Yolande's pale cheeks and her air of nervous tension.
But she couldn't let her down now. It was impossible –
not to be thought of!

At twenty-five past nine there was a knock at her
cabin door and Drina sprang out of the armchair. But it
was not Yolande; it was Yolande's stewardess, looking
concerned.

"I'm very sorry, Miss, but she says she can't dance.
She's sick and has a headache."

"Oh, but she *must* dance! We can't let everyone down
now, and think of all our work!" Drina was most
profoundly shocked and suddenly very angry. Yolande
just couldn't back out now. However nervous she felt,
she must go through with it. It was unheard of –
unthinkable –

"But she did warn you," said a voice in her mind.
"She did say that she thought she couldn't ever be a
dancer because of it."

"I'll come," she said quickly, snatching up her shoes
and bag. "She can't be really ill, surely?"

"Well, she looks quite bad, but she hasn't actually

been sick," the stewardess told her. "It can't be seasickness, anyway. It's as calm as can be, and she never turned a hair earlier on, when one or two people were sick. But she's shivering and looks very unwell. I've given her a hot water bottle."

"If you don't mind I'll go ahead quickly," Drina said and hurried down the seemingly endless corridor, through the gate, down three flights of stairs and along another corridor. She burst into Yolande's cabin.

Yolande was in bed, wearing blue and white pyjamas and looking very young and small. She shrank still further under the bedclothes when Drina stood above her.

"I'm s – sorry, Drina! Very sorry. I'm ill … I've got a cold. I never *meant* to let you down!"

Pity warred with a natural and healthy anger.

"I'm sorry if you've got a cold, Yolande, and I'm sorry if you feel ill. But do get up and dance, please. The concert will have started, even though they're always late with things." The professional in Drina came out with an indignant rush. "People always go on even if they're dying or their fathers are dead. They go on with broken arms and with temperatures of a hundred and three. Come on, Yolande, quickly! I'll help you to dress." But she knew, as she looked at the girl in the bed, that it was no use.

"I'm s – sorry. Your lovely dance. And – and I thought it such an honour to dance with you. But you can do it without me. It's *you* that the people want to see."

"I can't do it alone. It wouldn't have the same point. I'd have to alter it." But that was what she would have to do, and she would have to think quickly, too.

"I think you're hateful!" Drina flared and dashed out of the cabin, banging the door. A few minutes later she bitterly regretted that flash of unruly temper – the temper that her grandmother believed she had inherited from her Italian father. Yolande had looked so small and lost; clearly her problem was a bigger thing than Drina had supposed. But there had been so little time. Afterwards – afterwards she would go back and make amends, would do her best to forgive and understand.

But now there was only time to think about *Twentieth Century Serenade*. She stood in the hall on the Promenade Deck, visualising her created movements and trying to see how she could carry the whole dance alone. It would have to be done. She would have to improvise in places, that was all.

She almost ran through the main lounge, unaware that her flying figure was followed by some curious and interested glances, dashed through the writing-room and hesitated in the doorway of the ballroom. Someone with a rather uncertain baritone was singing a song. That must be Mr Carr, then. There was still someone else's piano solo.

She ducked back into the writing-room to sit down and put on her ballet shoes, and then – having thrust her other shoes under the chair – went shyly and still rather breathlessly into the big room. The Assistant Purser saw her and signalled to her to sit in one of the chairs reserved for the performers.

Walking forward to the front row, Drina did her best to look about her. Some of the lights were on and it was quite easy to pick out her grandparents in the third row and Catherine Colby and Peter Bernoise near the back. But she could not see Mrs Rossiter's smartly arranged grey hair, nor Grant's conspicuous fair head.

Her heart dropped like a stone. They weren't there! But they *must* be. It was just that she hadn't picked them out. In the front row she could see almost nothing of the audience, so could retain hope for a while.

She heard very little of the piano solo and encore, but rose at once when the Assistant Purser signalled to her. She said composedly to him. "Could you explain, please? My – my partner is ill. I shall have to dance alone, and – and improvise a little. The choreography is by me and the ballet is called *Twentieth Century Serenade*, the same as the music."

Once on the little stage she could see the whole audience, but she did not try to look for Grant. She waited while the orchestra played a few bars and then began to dance, moving slowly to the quiet, dreamy passages. Then she could think only of her ballet for two that was now a solo, trying to save its character and some of its meaning.

And it seemed that she succeeded, for at the end there was a burst of applause, far more spontaneous than for either of the two previous performers.

"Encore! Encore!"

Drina began to dance again at the point at which they had agreed, only now she had to do Yolande's solo as well as her own. She moved with her usual sureness and easy grace, her leaps so light and apparently effortless that Catherine Colby murmured to her husband:

"She's definitely a girl to watch. Her own choreography, too. Very simple, of course, but most effective, and absolutely right for the music. I think she'll go far."

"Dominick thinks so," said Peter Bernoise. "Though he sticks to it that one can't really prophesy. She's only about thirteen, I believe."

"No, she's nearly fifteen, though you would never think it. I don't believe that Igor Dominick need have doubts. If ever I saw promising material – "

If Drina could have heard them she might have found some comfort. But she couldn't hear and she knew by then that Grant was not there, nor were his father and mother. The fact that he hadn't been interested enough to watch her dance was, in its way, the bitterest thing she had ever experienced.

She stood there, smiling at the applause, wishing that she could run away, lock herself in her cabin and burst into tears.

She went back to her seat and sat through the one remaining item before the short interval. In the interval people crowded round her, praising her and asking about her dancing career. She answered politely but abstractedly and, as soon as she could, slipped away.

Her cheeks were burning and her eyes felt hot, too, and there was a strange, half-angry pain in her chest. How could she blame Grant for not bothering to watch a girl he thought a child dance? But he had called her a professional and at times he had seemed to like her. Yes, she *did* blame him. She almost hated him as she went back to the deserted covered deck, where it was draughty and now very cold indeed.

But she was not selfish or unkind and the memory of Yolande's stricken face was still vividly with her. Two people had let her down and it would be easy to be bitter about both of them. But the remedy, with Yolande at least, lay in her own hands. She knew that she must forgive the girl of whom she had grown fond during the few days since they had met. She felt curiously protective towards Yolande, wishing that there was some way in which she could help her over the awful problem of nervousness in front of an audience.

It was something that she had never quite met before, but that was not to say that she might never meet it again. It might – terrible thought – even happen to her, if she got run down or something happened to break her nerve.

"There, but for the grace of God, go I," Drina thought, as she had thought when Daphne Daniety was asked to leave the Dominick and on a good many other occasions.

With a rather set face she made her way back to Yolande's cabin, entering after the briefest of knocks. The light was on and Yolande was reading, or trying to read. She dropped the book with a little cry when she saw Drina. Her face was blotchy and her eyes extremely red.

"Oh, you've come to be angry again! But you can't be more angry than I am with myself. I *hate* myself! I don't know what it is – something awful takes possession of me. I *couldn't* have faced all those people, though I knew I was letting you down. I shall never try to dance again – I'll never be happy again!"

Drina dropped on to the bed and took one of Yolande's hands in a rare demonstrative gesture.

"What rubbish you talk! Of course you'll be happy again, and perhaps a lot sooner than you think. And you certainly are going to keep on dancing – before an audience, too – if it's the last thing I do. We'll find a way, I promise you that we will, though I know I've got so little time. You dance so well it would be a wicked waste, but you've certainly got to get over this thing, whatever it is. You'll have to fight yourself when the chance comes to dance in public again. You'll have to promise yourself that you'll do it."

"Oh, you are great! But it's easy to *talk*." Yolande was crying again.

"I know it is. But you can't let dancing go so easily when you show so much promise."

After quite a long time Yolande said in a muffled voice: "I will try if – if I get another chance. I think this has given me a dreadful shock – seeing what I can do to someone I like and – and admire. I nearly got up after all and followed you, but it was too late. Was it – was it awful? Was it spoilt?"

"Well, of course it was spoilt, but I suppose I was the only one who knew. People seemed to like it all right."

"Because you dance so beautifully."

"There wasn't really much competition," Drina said dryly, remembering the piano solo that, at the time, she had not realised she had been judging, and the narrative poem that had followed her own dance. "Now, look! Go to sleep, because we have to be up so early. Don't you want to see America? I shall go up on deck soon after half-past six. We're having breakfast at seven and then we have to see the immigration people, who are coming on board at seven-fifteen. You know where I shall be? At the Mandeller Hotel. And I've got your address and telephone number. We'll fix up about those classes."

"And you'll still come to tea? I thought – I thought you'd never want to see me again."

"I don't drop my friends so easily. I'd love to have tea with you, and perhaps we can explore Greenwich Village. I'm sure you'll like your aunt. Is she meeting the ship?"

"Yes, she said so."

"Then you'll be all right."

And Drina squeezed Yolande's hand, said "goodnight" and set off on the long walk to her own cabin.

Once there she locked the door and flung herself on the bed, burying her face in her arms and shedding a few tears. It seemed so sad that it should end like that, and probably she would not manage to see Grant in the morning.

# 8

# Skyscrapers in the Morning

In spite of everything Drina slept well and it was after six o'clock when she awoke. Some of the sorrow had gone and she was filled with a tremendous astonishment. Already America must be there – it must be possible to see land!

She washed and dressed rapidly, putting the last of her possessions into her little overnight case and leaving her coat ready. The ship still seemed quiet, and there was no one in the corridor except for a distant steward laden with suitcases.

She had never once used the lifts since leaving Southampton and now she bounded up the stairs to the Main Deck, then to the Promenade Deck, turning unerringly towards the starboard side, where the coast of Long Island must surely be?

And it was there! Peering through the windows of the covered deck she could see in the misty half-light that there was land quite near – a point with trees on it and a flashing light, a line of buildings that looked like factories.

America! Land after so many days of empty ocean. It

was a very odd feeling indeed, and she thought:

"Now I know exactly how Christopher Columbus felt! How *all* the explorers felt – coming to an unknown country. Oh, I *must* be asleep and dreaming!"

But the great ship was moving on steadily, close to a line of buoys, and the unbelievable thing must be true – that in a very short time they would be in New York.

It was almost seven o'clock and she ran down to the restaurant and found her grandparents already at the table.

"Granny! Grandfather! I've seen America!"

Mr Chester laughed. "It does seem astonishing the first time. Well, order your breakfast and then perhaps we'll get through the immigration business quickly and you'll be able to go on deck. You don't want to miss the Statue of Liberty and the sight of the downtown skyscrapers."

"I don't think I want any breakfast. Just some coffee."

But that Mrs Chester would not allow.

"Rubbish! You must have something. It's sure to be an exhausting business leaving the ship and it's a very hot morning. It's going to be roasting in New York. So late in September, too. I had hoped it might be cooler by now."

Drina realised then that it had indeed been very warm on the usually draughty starboard side of the covered deck.

"I hope it is hot and sunny. The sun was just coming up – round and red, more like the moon. But it's very misty."

She ate some grapefruit and some toast, but could not manage any more. She had not seen the Rossiters come in, but perhaps – as well as seeing Manhattan – there might still be a chance of seeing Grant again. She tried to tell herself that she didn't want to see him, but it was no use.

It was deeply frustrating to have to wait about to see the immigration officials and by the time they were sitting on chairs in the main lounge, moving up the queue every few minutes, she was wildly restless. Mrs Chester was inclined to be irritable.

"We won't be any quicker if you *do* work yourself up, you know. You'll be worn out before the day's properly started."

The officials sat at tables, one at the head of each line of chairs, and at last it was their turn. Drina practically danced with impatience as the man looked at her passport and then clipped a slip of paper into it. She rammed the passport back into her shoulder-bag and cried to her grandfather, "Oh, please may I go now?"

"Yes, but just wait a second," Mr Chester said, putting a detaining hand on her arm. "We're likely to dock soon after half-past eight, but it will be a little while, I expect, before we're allowed ashore. We'll meet you in the main hall on A Deck immediately the gangways have gone down. Don't forget."

"And don't forget your case and coat," Mrs Chester added.

"I won't, honestly." And Drina flew off, racing as fast as seemed safe along the covered deck, where people were thronging the windows, up the stairs to the Boat Deck, and up again to the Games Deck. She was just in time to see the Statue of Liberty on the port side, already almost astern. The famous green lady stood there high above her little grassy island, just as Drina had seen her so often in pictures and she drew in her breath sharply.

The morning *was* hot and still a little misty, but the sky was blue and now there was land on either side. New Jersey and Staten Island, she supposed, on the left, and Long Island on the right. Manhattan – where was Manhattan?

Oddly enough, she had the Games Deck almost to herself, and she dashed across to the other side, to where she could see ahead. She could not stop an incredulous cry as the sight burst upon her. Though she was to see many other places, she was always to remember that first sight of Manhattan Island as the purest thrill of her life. There it was, like some fantastic lupin garden of high buildings, faintly coloured in the morning mist.

She found herself muttering, "It can't be real! Oh, it can't be real!" as she stared in incredulous wonder.

They were travelling fast, and soon the ship was heading up the Hudson River. Gradually they passed the downtown buildings, and others, further to the north, loomed up out of the mist.

"That's the Chrysler Building and that's the Empire State, once the highest building in the world," said a voice in her ear, and she swung round sharply, taken so unawares that for a moment her open delight and relief showed on her face.

Grant was standing there just behind her, with his left arm in a sling.

"I thought – I thought I wasn't going to see you again! And – what have you done to your arm?"

"It's my wrist, not my arm. I came up for a breather after dinner last night and somehow managed to slip. Boy! Did I take a *tumble*! It's a bad sprain. They thought it was a break at first. Such a lot of fuss and it meant that I missed your dancing. It was a real disappointment. I didn't even have a chance to send you a message."

Warm happiness filled her as she stared unblinkingly at the distant tapering tower of the Empire State Building.

"I thought – I thought you weren't interested."

"Interested? I guess I was very interested. I wanted to

see you dance. But as for seeing me again – you'll see us all. Sure you will. Didn't your grandparents tell you?''

''Tell me – what?''

''Why that you're coming to visit us at our apartment. Tomorrow evening, I think my mother said.''

''I didn't give them much chance to tell me anything. I – I was in such a hurry over breakfast and they wouldn't realise – '' But that was dangerous ground and she stopped abruptly, biting her lip and hoping that Grant wouldn't notice her heightened colour.

''Oh, how lucky I am!'' she thought. It was suddenly almost too much to be standing beside Grant Rossiter as the *Queen of the Atlantic* moved slowly towards the pier and to know that she would see him again. Now it was ten times more exciting to be nearly in New York. She cried:

''Oh, I know it's your own city, but don't you think it's wonderful? When I saw it just now down there – all those buildings in the mist – ''

''Sure I think it's wonderful,'' he agreed readily. ''I never get quite used to it, though I was born here. But you haven't seen anything yet.''

''I shall, though. I shall see all I can.''

They stood there by the rail looking down as slowly, slowly the *Queen of the Atlantic* moved into the quay. The air was hot and rather smoky and suddenly the sirens gave a startling, triumphant blast. Drina jumped and laughed excitedly.

Slowly, slowly the strip of water narrowed and she looked down a little dizzily to where the long covered gangways lay far below. They were being moved ... They were in place.

''I'll have to go!'' she said. ''Granny and Grandfather will be waiting, and I have to get my things. But I'll see you tomorrow.''

"Fine!" he said, almost sounding as though he meant it. "And I'm sorry about that dancing. Perhaps I'll have another chance."

"Not in New York," Drina said with regret.

She ran ahead down the familiar steps and stairs and shot past her grandparents in the hall on A Deck.

"I shan't be a minute!"

She burst into her cabin for the last time and snatched up her possessions. It was so hot that her hair was sticking to her forehead and she pushed it back. New York on a hot September morning ... the Rossiters' apartment on Central Park West ... Grant sounding as though he would be pleased to see her again. Oh, life was wonderful! More exciting than she had ever dreamed.

A few minutes later she followed her grandparents down the gangway into the vast Customs Shed.

# BOOK TWO
## Ballet in Manhattan

# 1

# First Day in New York

As it happened the whole business of dis-embarkation was not so trying as Mrs Chester had expected and within half an hour they were following a brawny porter up the Customs Shed to the exit.

"It can take such a long time at the worst," Mrs Chester said, with a sigh of relief.

"Granny, there's Yolande with her aunt!"

"Well, we can't wait now. We don't want to lose sight of our porter – "

But Drina had already darted forward and was plucking at Yolande's sleeve. She, and a very smart middle-aged woman, were also following a porter.

"Yolande! Are you all right? You've found your aunt?"

Yolande spun round, her face lighting up.

"Oh, Drina! Yes, this is my aunt – Mrs Dillon. Aunt Grace, here are Mr and Mrs Chester and Drina Adams, their granddaughter. They were so kind to me on the ship. I – I've asked Drina to tea."

While the adults talked briefly, but very cordially,

Drina noted with immense relief that Grace Dillon looked kind as well as smart. Yolande would probably be all right on that score, anyway.

"And, of course, I'll be delighted to see Drina any time," she said hospitably.

Drina felt very relieved as she followed her grandparents into the elevator and then into a bright yellow taxi.

They drove away from the docks, under an elevated highway and into shabby streets, with warehouses and flat-fronted houses that might have belonged to any English port.

"I always think that this part of New York is remarkably like Liverpool," Mr Chester said. "Even the elevated highway might be the old Overhead Railway."

But it wasn't Liverpool, it was New York. It was a New York taxi and the driver was disposed to be chatty. Drina was soon to learn that most New York taxi-drivers loved to talk and either told you their life story or quickly extracted yours.

She listened to his voice with some pleasure and pinched herself to make sure that she was really awake, and there. Really in New York on a hot and airless morning, on her way to the Mandeller Hotel.

It was only a short journey and soon they pulled up with a flourish at a hotel entrance on a broad, busy street. A blue-clad bell-boy began to assemble their luggage and Mr Chester paid the driver.

They took an escalator to a bright and very busy lobby on the next floor and Drina stood staring about her as her grandfather spoke to a clerk at the desk.

"A double room and a single were booked for me through American Express. Yes, Chester and Miss Drina Adams. Eleventh floor? Thank you."

Then they were in an elevator, shooting upwards,

and a few minutes later Drina saw her room, which was small but seemed to have everything she could possibly want, including a television, a radio and no less than four reading lamps. The lamps were on, even though it was very sunny in the room.

Mr Chester, who had accompanied her, tipped the bell-boy and then looked round.

"Your bathroom is through there. I think you'll be all right; it seems very comfortable and, being at the back, should be fairly quiet. Now come and see our room and I think we'll ring Room Service and order some coffee and perhaps some toast."

Her grandparents' room was very large. Drina wandered round examining everything, while Mrs Chester found her keys and began to open cases.

"Grandfather, as soon as I've had some coffee may I go out? Times Square and Broadway are very near. Couldn't I just go and – and get a first smell of New York?"

Mr Chester laughed, but his wife said quickly:

"Now, Drina, you can't go wandering about alone. You might get lost in a strange city. Wait till we've had a rest – "

It was Drina's turn to laugh.

"Oh, Granny, I won't. Get lost, I mean. I've learned the street map off by heart. I didn't get lost in Milan. After all, they speak English here. It isn't quite like a foreign city."

"Better wait until your grandfather has done his telephoning, and – "

But Mr Chester had other views. It was always he who stood up for Drina's independence.

"Well, I don't know. She's very sensible and she is used to cities. She's sure to have far more energy than we have, especially in this heat. I shall have a lot of telephoning to do, and I really think she might go and get a smell of things – as she so aptly puts it. She can come back here in time for an early lunch – say half-past twelve. But you will watch the traffic, Drina? Remember it's on the other side of the road from Britain."

"The same as Milan. I won't forget," Drina said gratefully.

"And you've got some American money?"

"Oh, yes. I used it sometimes to buy things on the ship. You know you could use either dollars or English money."

The coffee and toast arrived soon after that and then Drina unpacked quickly, put on something cooler and sallied forth with a tremendous feeling of anticipation. Down in the main lobby she was suddenly struck with an idea and went to ask if there were any letters for her. The clerk put her hand in a pigeon-hole and brought out three – from Jenny, Rose and Ilonka, as Drina saw with pleasure. But she put them into her shoulder-bag to be read later.

Outside, the humid warmth seemed to hang like a blanket, and, as Drina soon realised with amusement, "getting a smell of New York" certainly was appropriate for that particular part of the city. There were many small, rather scruffy foreign restaurants and the smell of various kinds of hot food was rather overpowering.

She sauntered slowly south, crossing 45th Street and stopping to look in a fascinating drugstore window. Crowds of people hurried up and down and she looked at them with interest just because they were New Yorkers, though in appearance they differed little from a similar crowd in, say, Soho.

Then she turned east on 44th Street, which was almost deserted and blessedly shadowy. But the quietness and shade didn't last for long, for soon she was in Times Square, where the sunlight was dazzling and the noise, crowds and traffic were considerable. She drew back against a shop window and stood there with her hand on her shoulder-bag, drinking it in. It was garish, but it was fascinating, and there were so many cinemas and theatres within a small area. She walked on to read some playbills, thinking:

"This is Broadway. Perhaps someday I shall be dancing at one of the theatres here. If only *Argument in Paris* had done well in London it might even have come here. Heaps of British plays do." But *Argument in Paris*, the West End play in which she had once had a part, had been a rather splendid failure.

"Perhaps," she thought, as she went on, "*Diary of a Dancer* will come here. How wonderful that would be for Terza."

She glanced quickly at her street map and walked south again, arriving very quickly at 42nd Street, which was much wider and busier than most of the cross-town streets. The map told her that there were some gardens just behind the New York Public Library on 42nd Street so she went that way, crossing 42nd in a rush when the green light said "Walk". It would take a day or two to get completely into the habit of expecting the traffic to approach her first on the left. Though, in any case, many of the streets seemed to be one-way.

Bryant Park was small and filled with trees already turning gold and a few leaves were drifting gently down in the still air. She made her way to an empty seat and sank down triumphantly, feeling that now she had made her first contact with the new city.

Sitting there in the heart of Manhattan she opened Jenny's letter.

*I wonder where you'll be when you read this?* Jenny began. She had typed the letter quite creditably, though the words ran together here and there. *Somewhere in New York – how astonishing it seems! I don't believe I shall ever go further than London, and even that won't be very possible now.*

*Still, things might be worse, I suppose, though there are times when I feel ready to burst. Book-keeping is beastly and I don't seem to make much progress with shorthand, but typing isn't bad. Of course I sometimes used Father's typewriter, but they say I do it all wrong, using the wrong fingers.*

*On the whole they are a dull, rather silly lot – I can't help it, they are – but Timothy is nice and thoroughly open-air. He wanted to go in for forestry, but his father won't hear of it; says he wants him in his office. So in a sort of way we are fellow-sufferers. We talk a lot about the country and climbing. He says why don't I join the Youth Hostels Association and go hostelling at weekends. It's very cheap and it does sound fun. I think I may next year.*

*I went to the farm last weekend, though one side of me thought I ought to stay away. But I couldn't, and it was like coming alive again, though I won't say it to anyone but you.*

*We are moving into a smaller house, as someone has made a good offer for this one, and we are all managing pretty well considering.*

*Anyway, never mind my troubles. I shall think of you endlessly and mind you have a wonderful time. Don't get run over and please don't come back with an American accent!*

> Lots of love
> from
> Jenny

Then Drina read Ilonka's and Rose's letters, which were both packed with snippets of gossip from the Dominick and Chalk Green. Both schools seemed very far away, as indeed they were. She put the letters away, jumped up and walked briskly out of the park into 42nd Street.

As the day wore on she felt even more in a dream state than she had done on the *Queen of the Atlantic*. There was so much to take in ... the heat was so intense ... and, wonder of wonders, her grandfather had managed to get seats for the Metropolitan Opera House that very evening.

"I had to take these," he explained, when they were having lunch in one of the restaurants attached to the hotel. "They were three returns, I think, for they were booked up for the rest of the week."

"Tonight will be wonderful," said Drina. "But what about Yolande? We promised."

"Well, she wouldn't want to leave her aunt the first night. I also got four tickets for a Spanish ballet company at a theatre on Broadway for Thursday evening. You can tell her when you telephone."

"Drina ought to have gone to bed early tonight," said Mrs Chester. "We all had an early start and I don't want her ill – "

But Drina felt far from ill. She felt full of energy and could hardly bear to waste a minute.

When she telephoned Yolande, her new friend, too, sounded in quite high spirits.

"Oh, Drina, it's a beautiful little house! And I have a lovely room, with a television set of my own. And I do like Aunt Grace. She says she wanted me to live with her long ago, but it wasn't really possible when I was younger as she's been in business ever since her husband died. She has a shop on Fifth Avenue – the bottom part quite near here. I went to see it this morning. She sells the most heavenly expensive underclothes and she gave me a frilly petticoat, the nicest one I've ever had."

"Oh, I'm so glad you like it all!" Drina said happily. Then she told Yolande about her own day, and about the extra ticket for the Spanish ballet, and promised to telephone again the next morning.

That afternoon Drina and her grandparents took a taxi over to Fifth Avenue, leaving it by the Rockefeller Centre. The famous street looked beautiful in the blazing sun. The spires of St. Patrick's Cathedral, high and sharp against the blue sky, were still entirely dwarfed by the great office blocks all around, some white and shining, soaring up and up, so that Drina got a crick in her neck trying to look up at them. Highest of all just there was the upthrusting mass of the RCA Building, part of the Rockefeller Centre, but, looking south, they could see the Empire State Building on the corner of 34th Street and Fifth Avenue, tapering up into the sky.

"And we can stand on the top of that!" Drina marvelled.

"Oh, yes, any time, day or night. You must go tomorrow. I shall be at the Conference, but your grandmother will take you about."

"In this heat I shan't get very far," Mrs Chester remarked ruefully. "I never expected it to be like this in September and I find it very tiring."

They walked down the Channel – a broad passage between the shops, filled with flowers and cool, flowing water – and Drina gave a cry of delight as she saw the Rockefeller Plaza ... the encircling flags hanging limp and brilliant in the still air, the great waterfall behind the huge golden statue, the tables under green and white umbrellas in the Lower Plaza.

"Oh, isn't it lovely? And *look* at the RCA Building!"

"Seventy storeys, I think," said Mr Chester.

They went down the steps to the Lower Plaza and had tea under one of the umbrellas, and Drina was conscious of the sun burning her arms and the faint cool spray from the falling water.

"In winter they skate here," her grandfather told her. "In fact I believe it's due to start again at the beginning of October."

"But they *couldn't!* The ice would fry."

"Well, perhaps this weather won't last."

But Drina hoped that it would. The heat seemed to add to the magic of being in New York.

By the time they sat in the Metropolitan Opera House that evening the day seemed to have lasted for a very long time. So many new impressions; already so many unforgettable memories. Was it really only that morning that she had stood on the deck of the ship, watching the downtown skyline drawing nearer and nearer? Was it only that morning that she had said goodbye to Grant Rossiter and Yolande? Drina could hardly believe it.

"I think it's beautiful in a way," she said, looking around the great modern building with interest. "But I wish I could have seen the old one. It must have been very like Covent Garden."

"I believe it was," her grandfather said, rather absently, for he was tired and not much looking forward to having to watch *Giselle*, which had never been one of his favourite ballets, even in the days when Betsy was dancing.

"All those blessed Wilis!" he thought, staring gloomily at his programme. "So much blue light and so much agony for poor Albrecht. But still Betsy loved it, and I certainly shall never forget her 'mad scene'."

Mrs Chester was thinking of Betsy, too, remembering the times she had danced on the stage in front of her, remembering with a sharpness that seemed to belie the passing of so many years, exactly how she had looked as she bowed and smiled to a cheering, clapping New York audience. Then she glanced at Drina, now absorbed in her programme, and sighed. The years had certainly passed and now here was Betsy's daughter, already trying to insist that she was nearly grown up. Betsy's daughter, who had fought with every weapon she knew to be a dancer, too.

"I wish that Betsy could have lived to cope with her," she thought, for suddenly she felt old and tired and not really able to understand the pains and pleasures, the uncertainties and sudden awareness of adolescence. Mrs Chester would greatly have preferred an early night to sitting watching a French ballerina – however famous – acting out the tragedy of Giselle. Drina must know every step of the ballet, too: it was strange that she could still bring to it this obvious mood of waiting for something wonderful and important.

Drina did indeed feel just like that. She sat with tightly clasped hands, once she had absorbed the details on the programme, her straight black hair swinging forward a little, her mood divided in a strange way between a cloudy dreaminess and sudden moments of such sharp awareness that it almost hurt. The very seat under her at times seemed overpoweringly important, for it was a seat in a New York theatre – and not only in a theatre, but in the famous Metropolitan Opera House.

And when the lights went down and the familiar music started, she gave a faint sigh and slowly relaxed her tense back. It was true that she knew almost every movement that each dancer would make. It was true also that she knew every note of the music. But that didn't detract from her enjoyment; it added to it. Besides, no two performances were ever the same, and she had never seen the French ballerina before.

When the curtain rose there was the familiar set, with the two little cottages and the backcloth of hills and a distant castle. There was Hilarion ... Albrecht ... and now Giselle, emerging from the little house on the audience's left, smiling, eager. And so it went on, the familiar ballet. The touching little scene of the plucking of the flower petals; "He loves me, he loves me not." The village lads and maidens dancing ... the arrival of the hunting party, with proud Bathilde in brilliant scarlet velvet ... the bestowing of the necklace on shy, grateful Giselle ... the unmasking of Albrecht ... Giselle's gradual realisation that she had been betrayed. In mounting tension Drina sat forward in her seat, scarcely breathing. She had seen many famous dancers' "mad scenes", but it still always came as something exciting, moving and terrible. The music rising to a crescendo ... the swishing sword and the watchers drawing back in fear and horror ... the expression on the face of Giselle, her flying black hair. And then she was dead and the curtain came down, and once more Drina was back in her seat, a little dazed, completely enraptured.

"Oh, she was good, wasn't she? Better than Catherine Colby, perhaps. She certainly looked madder and all that black hair – oh, thank you for bringing me! I do hope you're enjoying it, too."

Her pleasure was reward enough, they thought, as they tried to sound as though they were enjoying themselves.

"Oh, you're not! It's selfish of me, really, but it does mean so much to me. *Giselle* in New York! I shall never, never forget being here. And there's always the faintest, faintest chance that some day it might be me. Dancing Giselle. Can you believe that I might?"

Mrs Chester scarcely wanted to believe it. In many

ways she would have been relieved, even at that late date, to be told that, after all, Drina would not make a dancer. But she couldn't possibly even hint as much, in the face of so much warm happiness.

"Of course I believe it. I think you'll follow Betsy."

"Never, never so good, of course. How could I be? But if someone could tell me now, with certainty, that I'd dance Giselle one day I could die happy."

"That would do a lot of good," said Mr Chester dryly, and then suggested that they should stretch their legs before the second act.

# 2

# Exploring with Yolande

They returned to their seats just as the house lights faded and Mr Chester prepared resignedly to watch "the blessed Wilis", wishing heartily that ballets were more often happy ones. Of course there were lively ballets – in his time he had seen most of them – but Drina rather seemed to prefer the heavily tragic ones. *The Rake's Progress*, for instance ... a horrible and thoroughly depressing affair to Mr Chester's mind, and yet Drina admired it greatly. He remembered how she had returned from Covent Garden full of admiration for the scene in the madhouse at the end and she had even said that one day she would like to dance the role of the Betrayed Girl. He hoped fervently that she never would; the whole thing must be thoroughly agonising for nearly every dancer concerned. Aurora in *The Sleeping Beauty* ... now that would be quite different. Or Swanhilda in *Coppélia*, and of course the Sugar Plum fairy.

The curtain rose on the dim, blue-lit stage, with Giselle's grave marked by a cross. Mr Chester folded his arms and settled down to bear as best he could the sufferings of poor Albrecht, a little cheered by the thought that Albrecht probably deserved all he got.

Drina, on the other hand, sank down again into pleasure and anticipation, and was soon feeling deep admiration for the dancing of Myrtha, Queen of the Wilis. The *corps de ballet* was good, too; so much quiet menace.

But, as the long second act went on, her attention most unusually wandered. Or rather she slipped deep into her own thoughts, carried there, perhaps, by tiredness and by the familiar music. She was back at the rail of the *Queen of the Atlantic* that morning, standing there with Grant and hearing his quiet, drawling voice. Then she slipped further back to all their other meetings, remembering his face, the way he had looked playing deck tennis, the things he had said to her; casual, most of them, but extraordinarily important because *he* had said them.

Tomorrow evening she would see him again. That was wonderful, but suddenly it came to her, that, in a way, it would only prolong the agony. For now *that* might be the last time. It almost certainly would be. But at least she would be able to visualise him in his home, would have added a few more pictures to her meagre store.

It did seem so unfair to have to like someone who would so soon be over three thousand miles away across the Atlantic Ocean. And yet – she suddenly sat up sharply, quite unaware of what was happening down on the big stage. She was not wholly a dreamer; there was a practical streak, and she asked herself coldly what good it would really have done her if Grant had lived in London. She had never expected to fall in love before she was fifteen but it was clear enough that nothing could have come of it, wherever Grant had lived. Dancing was her life and must be for many years to come. There was not really room for an overpowering outside emotion. She knew that she must somehow accept it for what it was – a half-painful, half-lovely new experience in a, to her, romantic setting.

When she brought her mind back to the ballet it was almost over. Dawn had come and so Albrecht was safe. Giselle was moving slowly towards her grave.

"Very good dancing," Mrs Chester said briskly, as the lights went up and people began to hurry towards the exits. "I thought that the members of the *corps de ballet* were all excellent."

Drina felt rather ashamed that she had missed so much of the second act. It had never happened to her before, and was one more indication, if she needed one, that she just could not stay in love. She wondered what her grandmother's reaction would be if she said:

"I scarcely saw the second act. I was thinking about being in love." Mrs Chester would be surprised, to say the least. But surely it was easier thought than done? Falling in love was one thing; falling out of it again not easily achieved.

When they came out into the hot night people were gathered around the lighted fountain, and all the great buildings of Lincoln Centre were floodlit. Drina could hardly be torn away.

There were no taxis, so they took the bus south on Broadway to Times Square. When the brilliant lights of the square came in sight she cried out excitedly:

"Oh, isn't it marvellous? Far more brilliant than the West End! They ought to call Broadway the Great Coloured Way."

"It's very garish and vulgar," said Mrs Chester, as they pushed their way through the crowds.

"I did think so this morning, but I love the lights."

"It's only this part of Broadway that's called the Great White Way," Mr Chester remarked. "Broadway goes on for many miles, you know. It starts down in the Wall Street area, near Battery Park, and goes north into the Bronx, I think – beyond Manhattan Island."

"Yes, I saw it on the map," Drina said promptly, and he laughed.

"What a girl you are for maps, and you're good with them, too."

At last Drina was alone in her room and she wandered about switching on lamps, fiddling with the controls of the television set, running the bathwater slowly. She was tired and yet not sleepy; she felt as though it was an utter waste of time to go to bed when New York probably never wholly slept.

But in the end she lay down in silence and darkness, and surprisingly soon she drifted into a deep sleep.

In the morning she called Room Service and ordered her breakfast and then bathed and dressed quickly, eager for the day.

Mr Chester went off to attend the first session of the Conference and Mrs Chester, though looking tired, seemed prepared to go out fairly soon.

"I've just heard on the radio that the temperature in Times Square is eighty-nine," she said, with a sigh. "So early, too. What will it be like later in the day? I think we'd better go right over to Saks in a taxi and buy you those new dresses, and then I'll see how I feel. Why don't you telephone Yolande and ask her to meet us at Saks about half-past eleven? If she stands by one of the main doors, just inside the shop, we're sure to see her, and then, if I don't feel like it, I suppose you can go off on your own."

Yolande sounded very pleased by the suggestion. "Oh, I'd love to, Drina! Aunt Grace has gone to the

shop, and she said I could go there later if I liked, or else go out with you. She's given me plenty of money and told me to take taxis until I get more used to things."

Mrs Chester and Drina got a taxi outside the hotel and were soon on their way across town. Saks turned out to be a wonderful shop and Mrs Chester had quite a job to get Drina beyond the first counters, which held costume jewellery and silk scarves.

"Oh, Granny, I must take Jenny a scarf or a brooch. And then there's Rose and Ilonka and Miss Whiteway."

"I should do your shopping in a cheaper place," Mrs Chester said dryly, urging her towards the elevators. "Come on, Drina. Do you want your new dresses or don't you? At least it's blessedly cool in here."

Drina did want the dresses. She was already looking forward to wearing one of them that evening, and in the end she found almost exactly what she had hoped for: a pretty emerald green dress, with a full skirt, and a primrose yellow one that made her brown skin look darker than ever. The price of each was startling, but Mrs Chester scarcely turned a hair.

"I promised you and at least you don't outgrow things as soon as they're bought. That green one is really very pretty, though perhaps rather old for you."

Drina thought it was just right and she was in the seventh heaven as they went down again, clutching the attractive boxes.

Yolande was there, wearing a pretty spotted dress and Mrs Chester eyed her with approval, thinking that she was clearly a nice child, with excellent manners, though it was a pity that she looked so pale and nervy.

She came to a quick decision, as they stepped out into the glare and almost overpowering heat of Fifth Avenue.

"I think that you young people can definitely go

exploring on your own. I just haven't the energy. I shall go and have a quiet cup of coffee and read a newspaper, and then I'll go back to the hotel, have lunch and rest this afternoon. Where were you thinking of going?"

Drina looked at Yolande and then laughed.

"Oh, Granny, there's so *much*. The Empire State Building, and Central Park, and the Museum of Modern Art – I do want to see some of the paintings there. There's the Metropolitan Museum of Art, too. They have a whole room full of Degas paintings. And Yolande loves Degas, too. Then there's Greenwich Village, where Yolande lives, and – "

"You sound as though you'll have enough to keep you going for some time," Mrs Chester remarked.

"I want Drina to come to MacDougal Alley and have tea with me," Yolande said eagerly.

"But what about lunch?" Mrs Chester asked.

"Oh, we'll have something somewhere," Drina said confidently. "We'll be quite all right, honestly. We won't starve."

"Aunt Grace telephoned about the ballet classes," Yolande said, rather shyly. "I'm to go tomorrow afternoon, and Aunt Grace asked if Drina could go, too, a few times, and Madame Lefeuvre was delighted. She's French, really, but she spent some years in London. She knows all about the Lingeraux and the Dominick. Aunt Grace just loves to talk and she told Madame all about how Drina danced Little Clara at the Edinburgh Festival, and about the ballet she did for the ship's concert … " Her voice faltered for a moment; it was a painful memory.

"I don't see how either of you can think of dancing in this heat."

But Drina laughed. "The school is probably air-conditioned and I do want to go, Granny."

"Oh, very well. You'll please yourself as usual, I suppose. Well, I'll take the parcels with me and I'll expect you back at the hotel not later than half-past five. We're expected at the Rossiters' apartment at seven, and you'll want a bath and change. Mind you get a taxi all the way up from Greenwich Village."

"I will, Granny," Drina promised meekly, and she and Yolande set off together down Fifth Avenue, heading south to where the Empire State Building tapered upwards in the blue haze.

"You didn't ever tell her about – about why I didn't dance on the ship?" Yolande asked, with an anxious sideways glance. "I – I told Aunt Grace I wasn't well."

"Of course I didn't. I won't ever tell a soul. It's our secret."

"Promise?"

"Of course I promise," Drina agreed readily.

They dawdled along, looking in shop windows, but always drawn onwards by that immensely high building on the corner of 34th Street. As they went Yolande told Drina more about her aunt and the little house in MacDougal Alley.

"She really is nice. I knew it at once and it was such a relief. And the shop's really lovely; everything's fabulously expensive. She's got an assistant called Elizabeth; she's nice, too. And another one called Mamie. *She's* only eighteen and very pretty. Elizabeth is really Miss Blenkopp and she's quite old and sort of stiffly smart. Not the frilly kind. I love MacDougal Alley. I never thought that there'd be anywhere like it in New York. I thought that everyone lived in skyscrapers, in apartments. The Alley is a little private road, rather like a Mayfair mews, with funny old lamps and trees."

"I'm just longing to see it. It is a bit surprising about the skyscrapers," Drina admitted. "I really believed there'd be lots more of them, but so many of the buildings are quite low and ordinary. Won't it be thrilling to go up the Empire State?"

"Aunt Grace said we wouldn't get much of a view today; it's so misty."

"Still I want to do it quickly. If we look down on things we'll understand so much quicker. Fancy! A hundred and two storeys, isn't it? But the World Trade Towers are higher."

They crossed Fifth Avenue and presently approached the main doors of the Empire State Building. Inside it was dark and cool and they walked a little timidly along a long, broad corridor to buy their tickets. There were a few other people doing the same thing and they all crowded into an elevator. The elevator moved so swiftly and smoothly that it was scarcely possible to know that they were moving, and in no time at all they were very high indeed and changing elevators to go on a few more storeys to the observation platform.

When they left the second elevator their ears were singing a little and they stood still to stare about them. There were a few stalls that sold postcards and souvenirs, and a little café where drinks and sandwiches could be bought. But both were really only anxious to get outside, to see that fabulous view.

And it *was* fabulous. They stepped out into the blaze of the sun and looked over the nearest parapet. And there lay New York far below, perhaps all the more impressive because of the faint haze ... streets and buildings seen as though from an aeroplane and –   "I can't believe it!" Drina said after rather a long time, finding the words only with difficulty. "Ever since I left London I haven't felt like me at all, and this just – just clinches it. Could you pinch me, do you think? Hard!"

Yolande obeyed and the pinch was so remarkably

painful that Drina was forced to accept her own reality and the reality of the scene.

"I suppose I *must* be here, then. And it's the most wonderful thing I've ever done in my life."

Yolande was looking at the little folder they had been given. "We're looking east, aren't we? Then that's the East River and Brooklyn – "

"And the United Nations – that great building by the water, like a great flat box. Over there to your left. And look!" Drina pulled her round until they were gazing north. "That's the Chrysler Building; it looks rather like this one. There, not very far from the UN. And that must be the RCA Building; we were right by it at Saks. And the park and the lake and just a glimpse of the George Washington Bridge over the Hudson. Like a ghost bridge; I do wish it wasn't so misty." Drina stared and stared, enraptured and still half-unbelieving.

"It's very thrilling!" said Yolande. Her cheeks were quite pink and her eyes were shining. "I think that some day I may be glad to live here."

"It's beautiful and exciting and incredible all at once," Drina said thoughtfully. "I do believe I envy you. I never thought I could. I never thought I could feel about any city as I do about London. But there's something about New York ... I felt it at once. I could love it. I love it now. I shall want to come back."

"Do you think you ever will?"

"I might. I shall *have* to." And now she was not thinking of Grant. "It's sort of got me, just in twenty-four hours. I expect that people always love it or hate it. You couldn't be indifferent to it."

"But still it's awful to think I may never see England again," Yolande said, with a faint quiver in her voice.

"But you will. Your aunt has plenty of money, hasn't she?"

"She seems quite well off," Yolande admitted. "And *I've* got some money. Or I shall have when they've sorted out my London aunt's affairs. She left me everything, including the house, which is going to be sold."

"Then there you are. Only lack of money might have stopped you, and meanwhile you've got all this. All the rest of America, too; you never know where you'll go. But I have to sail away again a week on Saturday." It was a curiously bitter thought, even with the Dominick and all her friends in London. For the moment they all seemed very far away and surprisingly unimportant. "My mother loved New York. She often danced here," Drina added, without thinking.

Yolande stared.

"Your mother? Was she a dancer, then?"

"Yes," Drina said hastily. "She danced with the Dominick ages ago. She died when I was only eighteen months old. Come and look round the west side. I believe I can see the *Queen of the Atlantic*, still at the pier. Yes, there she is! And look! That's New Jersey across the Hudson River."

They wandered round again until they were looking south, seeing the downtown skyscrapers in a close mass, with the East and Hudson Rivers hemming them in. Beyond was the Harbour, with the Statue of Liberty just visible in the thinning mist.

"There's another lift," Yolande pointed out. "We can go higher still."

So they went up to the topmost, glassed-in observatory, where it was so intensely hot as to be almost unbearable. After that they were so hungry and thirsty that they went down again to the open platform and Drina suggested that they should have coffee and sandwiches where they were. They munched and drank in great contentment and then took a final walk round, reluctant to leave that high place.

"It makes things – problems – seem sort of small," Yolande said, in a shy voice. "I think – when I'm miserable, or things get too difficult – I shall come up here."

"You won't be miserable any more, I hope," Drina said cheerfully, and they went down in two swift elevator rushes to the street again.

Yolande was hesitant about stopping a taxi on Fifth Avenue, but Drina stepped forward boldly and shouted "Taxi!" at the first empty one that came in sight. The driver grinned and drew up with a flourish and Drina said, "MacDougal Alley, Greenwich Village, please." For they had decided to go to Yolande's home and then to explore a little of the Village.

Drina was enchanted with MacDougal Alley and with Mrs Dillon's white-painted house tucked into a corner in the shadow of an old tree. She loved Washington Square, too, with its great arch and its row of delightful Georgian houses on the north side. Then they walked along Eighth Street, which was really the main street of Greenwich Village, looking into all the art shops. Here and there were pavement displays of paintings and it was all very fascinating. Finally, after exploring a good many hidden corners, they found themselves back on Fifth Avenue again, where it started near Washington Square, and that part was fairly quiet, with shady trees – quite a few dry leaves fluttering down – and big hotels.

By the time they wandered back along the north side of the square children of all ages were coming out of school, tumbling and laughing and being met by their mothers, and there were older students, too. Yolande explained that they belonged to New York University, which more or less dominated the square.

"Isn't it extraordinary?" Yolande remarked. "They're all Americans. This is America. And yet they don't look so very different. I think you'd better pinch *me*."

They went back to Yolande's new home and got the tea, for Mrs Dillon would not be home for some time yet. And gradually Drina grew restless and deeply excited, because in only a couple of hours now she would see Grant Rossiter again, and the apartment on Central Park West.

Driving back to the hotel in a taxi, with all the windows open and the hot wind blowing her hair about, she looked forward to the evening with that disturbing mixture of pleasure and pain.

Growing up, she thought, as the taxi stopped outside the hotel and she hastily counted out quarters and dollars, was really a most disturbing experience.

# 3
# Twentieth Century Serenade

The emerald dress suited Drina in quite a startling way, especially as she wore new white ear-rings and a white necklace with it. Mrs Chester rather disapproved of the ear-rings, but a precedent had been set in Milan and it was really too late to start protesting.

Besides, her husband disagreed.

"You can't hold her back, you know. And she is growing up so rapidly."

"But in some ways she looks so young. She's so small and slight. She could easily pass for twelve."

He laughed.

"My dear, she doesn't want to. What girl of nearly fifteen would?"

"I don't know I'm sure," Mrs Chester retorted. "They all seem to think they know everything nowadays."

Drina did not hear this conversation, and she felt very youthful and uncertain as they sped north towards the park. That was the *worst* of it; childhood seemed to be at war with something not yet fully known or understood.

It was another hot evening and the sky was luminous

and pale above the park, not yet ready for sunset splendour.

The entrance hall of the building where the Rossiters lived was very impressive, long and high, with marble pillars and ornate walls. There was a doorman in uniform who put them into the elevator and told them which button to press. They shot up to the tenth floor and were met by Mr and Mrs Rossiter. There was at first no sign of Grant, but as they went into a big, elegant room, with a shining polished floor, he appeared in the far doorway.

The adults were already deep in conversation and he only greeted Mr and Mrs Chester briefly, then turned to Drina.

"Hi, Drina!"

Drina, a little breathless to find him just as she remembered (though why should it be otherwise?), managed to gasp:

"Hullo!" She thought that Grant must think her both childish and foolish and she would have been very surprised if she could have read his thoughts as he had stood in the doorway for a moment.

"She is a pretty kid," he had thought. "Well, no, not pretty exactly, but striking, with all that straight black hair and those big dark eyes." And for a moment he had been filled with a quite surprising regret because she would soon be going away. He was remembering the look she had given him when he surprised her yesterday morning on the Boat Deck of the *Queen of the Atlantic* as he asked casually:

"How are you liking New York?"

"Oh, it's wonderful! I love it!"

"She and that girl she met on the ship have been around by themselves all day," Mr Chester remarked.

"And didn't get lost?"

"Oh, I couldn't!" Drina cried, shyness forgotten. "It's so very easy; the streets all numbered in order. We went up the Empire State Building this morning."

"You ought to go back again at night, or up the RCA Building. That's really something. I like your dress," he added, in a lower tone.

"Saks, Fifth Avenue," said Drina, with a grin, and he laughed.

"I guess I might have known. Are you going to turn into a New Yorker in just a week or two?"

"I wish I could," she said doubtfully. "I – I could feel it was my own city. Is that dreadful cheek?"

"No. We'll all be glad that you like it. It sure is some city, but plenty of people don't fall for it. People in England seem to have a peculiar picture of it in their minds. It isn't all thugs and gangsters, and noise and speed and hot jazz."

"It's beautiful. And parts of Greenwich Village are very, very quiet, really like a village."

"You ought to go to the Cloisters," Mrs Rossiter said, as they went in to dinner. "It's away up on the Hudson, beyond the George Washington Bridge."

"A – a sort of reconstructed monastery," Drina said eagerly. "With doorways and vaulting and tapestries from France."

"Well, just listen to that! She knows about it already. I guess she doesn't miss much."

"I've got a book – and a map." Drina was shy again.

"Well, we ought to arrange something before you go back."

And at that Drina was filled with wild hope. Not the last time, then? But would Grant go, too? After that she was very quiet, listening to the conversation with one part of her mind and watching Grant whenever she herself seemed unobserved, taking the old pleasure in everything about him.

The meal went on for a long time and Drina was warmly happy, not at all impatient to move. But when the coffee was finished, and the others were deep in conversation about current affairs, Grant rose.

"Why don't I show Drina the lights?"

"Yes, do," said his mother. "Our view at night is something very special."

Drina rose and followed Grant, and they went back into the room she had seen first. It was more or less in darkness, but Grant did not turn on any lights. He put his hand lightly on her arm and steered her to the far window, and in another moment Drina stopped dead, crying as she had cried when she had that first glimpse of New York:

"It can't be true! Oh, it really can't!"

Grant opened the window wide and they leaned out side by side. Away to the south the midtown buildings rimmed the park – a fairy view of thousands of brilliant lights, thrusting up into a sky that was clear and starry in its turn. Highest of all, a long beam swung round and disappeared, only to come round again as she stared in silent rapture.

"That's the light on the top of the Empire State Building," he said.

"A – a sort of beacon light?"

"The light of freedom. Did you see the poem on the observation platform? It really is something special, isn't it?"

"It's beautiful," she said softly. "I – I wish I could write poetry. Oh, you are lucky to live here!"

"Come to this other window and you'll see the park and the lights on Fifth Avenue on the other side. It runs right up past the park, of course."

"It's lovely," Drina said, seeing the lights reflected in

the dark lake, and the headlights of cars as they passed along the roads in the park. "But not like the other one."

"I guess you make your own poetry when you dance."

"I don't know. I wish I could think so. Some day I might make a ballet with a backcloth like this and very modern American music."

"I forgot that you were a choreographer, too," he said, with such respect that, for some reason, she came tumbling down into childishness again.

"I'm not. I've only made one little dance. I – I've such a lot to learn."

Soon after that they went back to join the others and for the rest of the evening she had no chance to talk to Grant alone. But she was very happy, and happier still when she heard plans being made. The Rossiters were to go and have dinner at the Mandeller Hotel on Saturday evening and something would be arranged about going up to the Cloisters.

As they sped back through the evening traffic, she was tired and very silent, astonished by the sheer excitement of life. New York for a week and a half yet ... dancing tomorrow ... so many things to see ... Grant ...

"You're worn out," Mrs Chester said, rather anxiously. "Get to bed quickly and have a good night's sleep."

But Drina lay awake for over an hour, not wishing to sleep. There was far too much to remember and to hope for in the immediate future.

Before she left for Madison Avenue the next afternoon Drina wrote to Rose.

*Oh, Rose, it's a heavenly city! So alive and friendly and exciting, and so beautiful, too, in the main, though of course there are lots of poor and scruffy parts. I even like them!*

*Last night we had dinner at an apartment on Central Park West and the view from there was like fairyland. A million lights glinting on black velvet!*

*This morning Granny said that she wanted to write letters (but really she doesn't like the terrific heat and is tired), and so I went out by myself. I went to look at Pennsylvania Station, which is between Eighth and Seventh Avenues, a few blocks south from here. You know how I love stations, but I never saw a single train! They are somewhere underground, and the same at Grand Central Station, so I'm told.*

*Now I'm going to meet Yolande Mason and we're going to a ballet class. Won't it be odd to dance in America? Granny doesn't approve, but I'm glad to have the chance of keeping in practice.*

*Give my love to everyone at Chalk Green, especially to the twins. Emily, Bianca and dear Petrouchka. I hope he's being a good dog and not bringing you too many mangled little corpses! England and the Dominick seem very far away just now. Oh, I am glad that I came! Some day you'll come, too, I know; when you're dancing with the Dominick.*

> *Love from*
> *Drina.*

At four o'clock Yolande and Drina met in Madison Avenue, outside the dancing school, and went in rather shyly. But they need not have worried. Someone showed them the cloakrooms and changing rooms and, as they changed into practice costumes and put on their ballet shoes, many of the others talked to them. There was a pretty fair girl called Marilyn, who had been dancing since she was nine and who hoped to make ballet her career. She read all the ballet magazines she could lay hands on and knew about the Dominick and Lingeraux Schools.

There was a dark, Spanish-looking girl called

Mercedes, and two sisters from Brooklyn who were not twins but very much alike, with chestnut hair and green eyes.

They all crowded round, so friendly and interested that once more Drina thought that New York must be the friendliest city on earth. They swept Drina and Yolande up to the big studio on the third floor, where the advanced ballet class was to be held, and Yolande muttered anxiously:

"I oughtn't to be in the same class as you, Drina, but Madame seemed to think it would be all right. This is sort of Junior Advanced. She has a class for grown-ups at night."

"Of course it'll be all right," said Drina, looking about her with deep interest, but not finding much that differed from London, except the fact that Madison Avenue lay below, with Fifth Avenue only a block away, and not the tree-filled Red Lion Square.

Madame Lefeuvre was small, dark and rather elderly, but age had made little difference to her dancer's body – she was still as slim and supple as a girl. She greeted the two Londoners with warm pleasure.

"How do you do? This is Yolande Mason? And you're Drina Adams? Yolande, of course, I'm to have with me for some time, but I'm very glad that you've come to me while you're in New York, Drina."

"I thought it would be fun, and – and very interesting," Drina said. "And I hate to get out of practice."

"That is very wise of you. How do you like New York?"

Once more Drina said that she loved it, and her tone carried such conviction that Madame looked satisfied.

"I love New York, too, though I was very fond of London. Well, now, everyone to the *barre*." And soon after that the class started.

It was always of great interest to Drina to observe different teaching methods and a different manner, and she soon learned to respect Madame Lefeuvre. She seemed a person of enormous authority and had a very high standard. Some of the girls in the class were soon looking flushed and rather unhappy, but Drina and Yolande came in for no criticism while they were at the *barre* and Madame also left them alone during the centre practice that followed.

After a time, though, she told everyone to rest and turned swiftly to Drina.

"Mrs Dillon told me that you danced on the *Queen of the Atlantic*. That you composed a ballet for yourself and Yolande, but that Yolande was unwell and so you danced alone."

Drina flushed, suddenly shy.

"Yes, Madame. But it was only a little ballet to *Twentieth Century Serenade*. The – the first I've ever done."

"We could perhaps see it now? You and Yolande will dance for us? The pianist can play *Twentieth Century Serenade*. You have the music?" And she turned to the girl, who nodded.

Drina never minded dancing in front of people as a rule, but she saw Yolande's face and her sudden tension.

"Oh, please, I would sooner not. I – I think I've forgotten it already."

Madame gave her a shrewd, faintly puzzled look.

"Nonsense! How could you forget? And it would give us all great pleasure. Drina Adams," she said, turning to the curious, watching girls, "danced Little Clara in *Casse Noisette* at the Edinburgh Festival with the Igor Dominick Company."

"I guess we'd love to see it!" Marilyn said eagerly.

Yolande gave Drina an anxious look, but it seemed impossible to refuse any longer. Drina mumbled:

"I'm afraid we'll have to, but it'll be all right. She can't say very much, even if she thinks it awful."

Yolande, clearly wishing that she had never mentioned the matter to her aunt at all, nodded unhappily and they took their places, Drina saying rather shyly:

"It hasn't really got a story, but it is meant to be a twentieth century serenade. Two young girls, who at first aren't very much aware or alive, but who suddenly wake up and enjoy the century they live in."

The pianist was good and the familiar, lilting music began. After a few bars they started to dance, and very soon, as so often happened, Drina had forgotten all about the audience and was just enjoying herself, lost in the dance she had created. When the time came for Yolande's little solo she stood to one side, noting that her new friend was dancing remarkably well. Evidently she, too, had forgotten the audience, and Drina felt much relieved.

Her own solo followed and then the final concerted movements of the ballet. There was a little silence when they had finished and then the class applauded noisily. Madame, leaning on the piano, nodded.

"Ver–y interesting. Yes, very interesting indeed. A future choreographer, I have no doubt. Of course there are a few little faults, but on the whole it fits the music to a quite remarkable degree. You'll still be here a week today? Thursday evening of next week?" she shot at Drina.

"Oh, yes, Madame. Until the Saturday. We sail on the *Victoria* then."

"Good! Then that will be all right. Next Thursday the

whole school is taking part in a charity performance at the Carne-Lucas Theatre just off Broadway. For various reasons it was necessary to postpone it from the beginning of this month and now, unfortunately, we are one item short, as three of our best dancers – sisters – have moved to California. Your little ballet would be excellent, and there's still time to have it put on the programme. They have only just gone to the printer. You would be willing, you and Yolande?''

Drina hesitated, not knowing what on earth to say. The suggestion appealed to her strongly, for it would be lovely to dance in New York, if only at a show given by a dancing school, and it would at least be in a real theatre. But swiftly came all the painful memories of that evening on the *Queen of the Atlantic*. Yolande had said that she thought she would never let anyone down again, that she had learned a lesson. But was it true?

It would, of course, be a wonderful way to make sure, and she had said that she would help Yolande to overcome her fear. It seemed almost as though fate had stepped in, and yet – was it possible to trust Yolande? Was it even fair to force her to make such an effort? Or even to risk upsetting Madame and spoiling the show?

Yolande was pale and silent, and Madame turned to her, once more looking rather puzzled.

''Would your aunt object, Yolande?''

''Oh! Oh, no, Madame. At least – '' Yolande stammered and looked even more uneasy and unhappy.

''Then will you do that for us?'' No answer from Yolande so she went on: ''It is a most worthy cause and people always support our shows well.''

Yolande said suddenly:

''Yes, Madame. I will if – if Drina would like to.''

Madame turned back to Drina with that slightly

birdlike glance of enquiry, and she could only nod, wishing that she had had a chance to speak to Yolande in private first.

"Yes, thank you. If – if you're sure that my ballet's good enough."

"We will rehearse. And then there's the question of costumes. What had you in mind?"

"Well, on the ship, we couldn't do much. I – I wore a white dress – very soft and full – and Yolande was to wear pale green."

"Yes. Well, stay behind and we'll take your measurements. Something can be made very quickly. Something very simple. Both in white, perhaps, and with a dark curtain. We can't manage much scenery."

Drina listened to her, half-appalled, feeling that fate had certainly taken command. A good deal of anxiety settled on her heart.

# 4

# Trusting Yolande

By the time they were ready to leave the other members of the class had gone. Yolande scarcely spoke while they were changing, but once they had stepped out into the hot and breathless early evening air on Madison she burst out:

"Oh, I was silly to tell my aunt anything about it! It somehow just slipped out and she was so interested. Of course she doesn't know what – what really happened, and you promised not to tell."

"I know. I haven't forgotten."

"I never *dreamed* that anything like this would happen but now it has I shall have to do my best, however terrified I am. You do believe that, Drina? You do trust me?" Her face was very pale.

"Yes, I do," Drina said firmly, feeling it impossible to let Yolande even suspect the deep uneasiness that filled her. If that uninformed audience on the ship had terrified Yolande so much, how much worse might she feel in a real theatre, with an audience of "ballet mothers" and others interested in dancing?

"I'll do it. I really will. I'll dance just as well as I can and make your lovely ballet a great success."

"Of course you will. And now we'd better get a taxi and scoot back to the hotel," Drina said quickly. "Don't forget that we've got to have dinner before we go to the Spanish Ballet Company."

"How lovely to be going to *watch* dancing," Yolande said, with a faint sigh.

She cheered up during the meal, which they had in one of the restaurants attached to the hotel, and she was chattering quite eagerly as they walked the short distance to the theatre on Broadway. The performance started fairly late, so it was dark by then, with all the thousands of coloured advertisements making the street as bright as day.

The company was one that Drina had never seen before, but Spanish dancing always delighted her, particularly the sharp clicking of the castanets and the thrilling beating of the men's heels on the stage. The settings were brilliantly colourful and so were the women's dresses, which whirled and swayed as they danced.

"Do you think them good?" Mr Chester asked, during the intermission, and Drina frowned a little.

"I'm not really a judge of this sort of dancing, Grandfather. Quite good, I think, though it's a strange mixture of folk things and more 'stagey' numbers. I think the men are better than the women, and the dresses are pretty but rather 'stagey', too. I've seen lovelier ones, that really looked as though they were made of satin and brocade, not just stage costumes."

"Well, it's certainly more to my taste than *Giselle*," he said, smiling. "It seems to me very lively." And Drina was relieved that both he and her grandmother seemed to be enjoying themselves.

She had had a rather irritated little scene with her grandmother before they left the hotel, over the fact that she had promised to dance at the Carne-Lucas Theatre. Mrs Chester had been very annoyed, saying that it was

quite unnecessary and surely Drina could have managed without dancing for just a week or two? It would mean rehearsing in the heat, for one thing, and she had wanted Drina to have a real holiday. There would be tears and trouble if she were ill when she got back to the Dominick.

"But honestly, Granny, I shall love it. I do so want to dance in New York, and I'm not in the least likely to be ill," Drina had insisted, and had thought guiltily how much worse her grandmother would have felt about it had she known about the very real problem of Yolande.

One side of her did, in fact, wish quite heartily that they had never been invited to dance, but the other and far more vigorous side was sure that it would be all right. Her thoughts had flown almost at once to the realisation that Grant could see her dance. If, of course, he had really meant it when he had said that he would like to.

"I shan't leave Yolande for a single minute that day," she thought, as the Spanish dancing started again. "I shall simply shadow her and take her to the theatre by force, if necessary."

Towards the end of the performance her thoughts stole to Grant Rossiter once again, and she sank into the sheer pleasure of remembering all their former meetings, savouring every word that had been said. On Saturday she would see him again, and then perhaps again, so there was as yet no need to dwell on the sadness of going away. Meanwhile there was New York and dancing … She came to with a guilty start to find that the dancers were gathering for the final ensemble.

"I really am getting dreadful," she told herself. "When have I ever before not watched every single minute of a performance? I shall have to stop this."

Mr Chester insisted that, as it was so late, they must

all see Yolande home, and they sped south to Greenwich Village and then north again up the lighted avenues, not talking much. It seemed natural to Mr Chester that Drina should be quiet after such a long, crowded day, but Mrs Chester thought otherwise.

"I can't understand it," she said, when they were alone in their room. "Drina seems different to me. She's always had her dreamy side, but now there's something else. I've thought so almost ever since we left Southampton."

"You're imagining it, my dear."

"I'm not," she said vigorously. "Oh, well, perhaps it's just that she's so carried away by the new experience. It's certainly been a success bringing her to New York. She's a good traveller."

"She's an intelligent, open-hearted one, ready to like new people and appreciate new places."

"Appreciate? She falls in love with them, it seems to me. She always exaggerates everything so. I never knew anyone so carried away by beauty and strangeness."

"Her mother was much the same."

"Betsy?" Mrs Chester frowned. "Was she? Perhaps I'm forgetting. And I was younger then and maybe took it more for granted. Do you know, there were actually tears on Drina's lashes when they came back from seeing that view at the Rossiters."

"Well, it is something very special. I never quite get used to New York myself. There are so many aspects of it that hit one literally between the eyes."

"I wish it wasn't so hot," Mrs Chester said and went to adjust the air conditioning.

On Friday evening, when an early night was sternly insisted on by her grandmother, Drina sat up in bed writing to Jenny.

*Dear Jenny,* she wrote, with the pad balanced on her raised knees, *I hope you get the postcard I sent you yesterday of the view from the Empire State, but I've just got to write a letter, too. Thank you for yours. I read it in Bryant Park on my first morning here. It was so hot that 42nd Street just shimmered and the Chrysler Building nearer the East River almost seemed to sway in the blue haze.*

*It is wonderful here, but I feel so guilty and sad that I'm here and you are having such a beastly time, in spite of Timothy. Surely things must get better for you? Life couldn't be so dreadfully unfair forever? I do think that you're very brave. I know I couldn't be.*

*I could never, never grow tired of New York. I love the country since being at Chalk Green, but I'm really a city person through and through and it gives me enormous satisfaction to get to know another city. Everyone is very friendly; the people in shops and taxi drivers and the hotel people. They talk and talk and sometimes they ask about England. I think they have very good manners, too. They never bark "Sorry!" but always say "Oh, excuse me" and if you thank them for doing anything they say "You're welcome!" which I love.*

*This morning Grandfather didn't have a session of his Conference, so he and Granny and I went to the United Nations building down on the East River. It is a most wonderful place, and seeing it made the United Nations seem much more real and important. I don't think I ever really took it in before, but now when I hear them talking about the General Assembly and the Security Council I shall remember being there. It looks splendid outside, I think, so high and flat and boxlike against the sky.*

*We had lunch at the UN and then went right across town to catch a little boat that sails all the way round Manhattan Island. That is, Granny and I did, and Yolande met us and came, too. It was just marvellous, because the heat haze lifted*

*and everything was sharp and blue. We sailed right round the
Statue of Liberty, very close, and then swept towards the East
River. I think that the view of the downtown skyscrapers from
the water is one of the very best things. I can't believe it's real.
That's a feeling that I suffer from a lot. We went under all the
bridges – Brooklyn and Manhattan and Williamsburg – and
through the Harlem River and out into the Hudson River
again. It was lovely up there, quite countryish, and we saw the
Cloisters high up above the river. It's a sort of reconstructed
monastery and we may go there by car later. Then we sailed
under the George Washington Bridge, which is very
impressive, and back past the pier where we landed last
Tuesday, and now I really believe that Manhattan is an island!*

*Afterwards Yolande and I had to rush to Madison Avenue
for a class and rehearsal. Isn't it incredible? I'm going to dance
in New York! It's only an amateur thing, given by the dancing
school, but it's in a proper theatre and Madame has a very high
standard. Yolande and I are doing a ballet that I made up on
the ship.*

*It seems amazing that I've only been in New York for four
days. I've seen so much and in some ways it feels so familiar
and real. In other ways it seems like a wild dream and I still
have to pinch myself. I'm black and blue!*

*We leave a week tomorrow, but I'm not thinking about that
yet.*

*Love,*
*Drina*

Not even to Jenny, her closest friend, could Drina have
told about her feelings for Grant Rossiter and how so
many of her thoughts lingered on him. Jenny *might*
have understood – it was she who sometimes talked
about when they were married – but Drina felt fairly
sure that her feelings were too complicated, and
perhaps too sentimental, for Jenny to understand.

Jenny was practical and not a dreamer; a warm, kind, intelligent girl who liked people and, usually, realism. Drina's yearning to be with Grant would surely be outside her understanding? Anyway, she wasn't going to try by letter, though some day, she might tell her all about it. Some day, when New York was thousands of miles away.

*Twentieth Century Serenade* was going well and had been greatly improved by one or two suggestions made by Madame. Two white dresses had been designed for them and were being made. They were a little like the ballet dresses worn in *Les Sylphides*, but with a softer, more clinging line.

Madame seemed pleased and Yolande was quite confident and cheerful for the most part. Drina hoped fervently that her friend had come out of her nightmare of doubt and uncertainty, and she certainly looked much better. She liked her aunt, was happy in Greenwich Village, and was making friends with the girls in their ballet class.

After that first class and their brief talk that followed, Yolande made no further reference to the danger of letting Drina down, and Drina was careful never to hint that she was uneasy. But she was not completely happy, and she continued to vow to herself that she would stay close to Yolande on the fateful Thursday.

But then, on Saturday evening, the Rossiters came to dinner and it turned out that Mrs Rossiter planned to take them to the Cloisters on Thursday afternoon.

"I'm afraid I'm busy early in the week," she said apologetically. "But on Thursday my husband says we can have the car and Grant will drive us. He's fairly free at the moment, because he doesn't start work until the Monday after that."

"That's very kind of you," Mr Chester said. "The Conference is over on Wednesday, so I'd be delighted to go, and I know my wife and Drina will be very pleased."

Drina was sunk in despair. Thursday! The day of the show!

"It's – it's the dancing show," she said faintly, and Mrs Rossiter looked interested.

"The show isn't until evening. Eight o'clock, isn't it?" Mrs Chester asked briskly. Then she explained to the visitors, "Drina is dancing in a show at the Carne-Lucas Theatre. She and her friend Yolande are doing that ballet that Drina made up for the ship's concert."

Grant looked across at Drina and said the words she had so longed to hear, "Say! So I'm going to see you dance, after all? That's great!"

"We must get tickets," Mr Rossiter said. "I guess we'd all like to go."

Drina was very pink.

"I – I got tickets for you all," she said, a little breathlessly. "I – I hoped –"

"But of course we'll come. And we'll get you back from the Cloisters in plenty of time for you to rest and have a meal. Shall we say three o'clock?" Mrs Rossiter asked, turning to Mrs Chester. "Why don't you come to our apartment just about three?"

"That will be very nice," Mrs Chester said, rather puzzled by Drina's expression.

Drina was, in fact, suffering acutely. She yearned to go to the Cloisters; knew that she could not possibly bring herself to refuse. It might be the very last time she ever saw Grant. And yet there was Yolande and the fate of the ballet. She would have liked to ask if Yolande could go, too, but that would be cheek and there might not be room in the car. Besides, if Yolande went she would probably have no chance to be alone with Grant.

She chewed the matter over all the time the adults were talking and still knew that she would go. She couldn't *bear* to miss it, and surely Yolande would be all right? She did seem so much happier and more sure of herself.

There was nothing to do but trust her, and there was always her aunt, who would surely see that she set off to the theatre in time. In fact, Mrs Dillon was going to the show.

But what if Yolande insisted that she had been taken ill again? What if she *made* herself ill with nerves at the very thought of dancing in a theatre? Drina shuddered, but pushed the thought away. She just couldn't refuse to go on the outing. She knew that she would look forward to it hourly until it came.

# 5

# The Outing with the Rossiters

The days seemed to pass with increasing swiftness and New York grew more and more familiar, but never less wonderful. Now Drina handled American money as though she had been using it all her life and even used American expressions without thinking about it.

"If you go home saying 'sidewalk' and 'elevator' and 'gasolene'," her grandmother remarked, "I'm afraid you'll get laughed at. You even said 'You're welcome' to me this morning."

"Oh, I shan't, Granny. I'll go back to 'pavement' and all the rest as soon as I'm back in London."

"Well, I must say you're adaptable. You wouldn't like to apply for American citizenship, I suppose?"

Drina grinned at the sarcasm.

"No, thank you, Granny. I guess I'll go on being British."

"I guess I'm very glad to hear it," Mrs Chester retorted smartly. "America is all very well, but give me Britain every time."

"I can't really judge America though, can I, when I've

only seen New York? And sometimes I do wish I'd been
born a New Yorker."

"You were nearly brought up a Milanese."

"I know. I thought of that when I was in Milan. I
suppose I'd have gone to the ballet school at La Scala.
How odd life is. It's all such a chance."

"There was no chance about Milan," Mrs Chester
said rather grimly. "Well, I suppose it was chance that
made your mother meet and fall in love with an Italian,
but I fought to keep you when you were orphaned."

Drina hugged her suddenly: a most unusual gesture.

"I'm glad you did, Granny. I wouldn't be a different
me."

But, all the same, she often felt a very different person
from the one who had left London so short a time
before. She had seen and experienced so much, and
then there was the startling fact of being in love. In
some ways it slightly spoiled the days in New York,
because she so often longed to be with Grant and
Thursday seemed a long way away, and yet in another
sense it had added immeasurably to her awareness of
everything around her.

The days were very crowded, however, and she did
not have so very much time in which to dream. She and
Yolande were together a good deal, wandering about
Greenwich Village or exploring other parts of the city.
Together they went down to Battery Park and then took
the ferry over to Staten Island; they were shown over
the Rockefeller Centre and went to watch the dancing
of the famous Rockettes; they walked in Central Park or
sat talking on shady seats, they went to the
Metropolitan Museum of Art and Drina was thrilled
with all the Degas paintings; they wandered along Park
Avenue and lingered in Grand Central Station. There
was always something exciting to do or see and their

energy, even in the continuing heat, never flagged.

As well as all this there were the ballet classes and rehearsals and the friends they were making at the dancing school. On Tuesday they went to tea in Brooklyn and on Wednesday to have lunch with Marilyn Schrön, who lived quite near Yolande in Greenwich Village.

Drina always enjoyed Yolande's company, for she was intelligent and often amusing, and it seemed sad that their friendship was to be short.

"I wish the Atlantic wasn't so wide," she said, as they crossed Washington Square on their way from Marilyn's. "You *will* write, won't you? I shall want to know how you get on, and little snippets about New York. I shall even want to know about the weather, so that I can visualise it."

"Oh, yes, I'll write," Yolande promised readily. "And you must write, too."

"I wonder if you'll go skating in the Rockefeller Plaza? I can't bear the thought of missing that. And think of Christmas. There's a picture in my guide book of the enormous Christmas tree they have there, surrounded by huge angels."

"But you'll have the tree in Trafalgar Square and the one in Westminster Abbey," Yolande said, with the wistfulness of the exile.

"I know. But I'd like to be *here* at Christmas, all the same."

Wednesday evening brought the dress rehearsal at the Carne-Lucas Theatre and, as usual, Drina was delighted to be backstage. The Carne-Lucas was quite a small theatre but very charming. It was comparatively new and the dressing-rooms were very up-to-date and cheerful, very different from some that Drina had known. Even the Dominick Theatre was rather inconvenient.

She took her mascot, Hansl, with her, and she stood the little cat as usual by her make-up box, looking at him rather thoughtfully as she set to work on her face. This was not the first time that Hansl had been in a New York theatre, that was certain, for her mother had taken him all round the world. It really was the strangest chance that made Elizabeth Ivory forget her mascot that night when she left the Dominick Theatre after a performance to fly to the States.

Yolande was very quiet and rather tense, but she said nothing, and their ballet went off very well. Madame was pleased with both of them and showed them a programme, which had a note explaining that Drina belonged to the Igor Dominick Ballet School in London. It also said that she had danced Little Clara at the Edinburgh Festival, and had had two parts in West End plays: in *Argument in Paris* and as Margaret in Barrie's *Dear Brutus*. Drina begged a few programmes for souvenirs and went back to the Mandeller Hotel in high spirits, fairly sure that all would be well the next evening.

But she still had an uncomfortable, rather guilty feeling that she ought to have played safe and arranged to spend the afternoon with Yolande. Yolande, however, had seemed to see nothing surprising in her going to the Cloisters with the Rossiters and had said that she would probably go and help at her aunt's shop.

"You aren't worried?" Drina had asked hesitantly, as they parted, and Yolande had replied:

"Not really. I don't like the thought of it, but I'll do it. Honestly, Drina, I won't let you down. That other time – oh, it was awful! I vowed it should never happen again."

Drina telephoned her on Thursday morning and was relieved that she sounded much as usual. There was not a great deal that she could say, so she contented herself with telling Yolande that she would telephone again when they got back from the Cloisters. She would have given a great deal to be able to warn Mrs Dillon, but her promise to Yolande made that quite impossible.

So, after lunch, she put on her new yellow dress and waited impatiently until it was time to leave. She kept on feeling little twinges of excitement, and she wondered, as she had done before, if Grant would still be the same. If you thought about a person a lot you might perhaps create someone quite different in your mind.

But when they stepped out of their taxi they saw Grant sitting close by in a large red car, and he looked just as she had imagined him – brown-faced, fair-haired, warm and friendly.

The doorman telephoned up to say that the visitors had arrived, and Mrs Rossiter came down very quickly. Drina found, to her immense pleasure, that she was to sit in front with Grant, and did not know that, looking at her eager, sensitive face, Grant was once more visited by a stab of regret because she was going away.

He knew very well that she was attracted to him and was pleased and flattered as well as rather touched. He had been popular with girls almost as long as he could remember and was never short of someone pretty to take out, but there was something about the black-haired, dark-eyed girl from London that stirred him in a way no one else had done. A pretty kid … more than that … perhaps a future ballerina. Grant appreciated ballet and had always been, he told himself, rather susceptible to Italian types. It was a pity that she was going away on Saturday, and yet perhaps it was just as well.

But none of this showed on his face as they sped north, presently taking the express highway beside the Hudson. He pointed out the Riverside Drive on their right and anything else he thought might interest her, and Drina sat with her hair blowing and her hands clasped, content just to be there, watching his hands on the wheel and his intent face as he steered through the traffic.

It was beautiful near the river and even lovelier when they were amongst the trees of Fort Tryon Park, climbing upwards towards the Cloisters.

The car was parked high above the river, where there was a splendid view up and down stream and over to New Jersey. Drina leaned on the wall, above the trees and bushes that were already taking on the golds and yellows of autumn, and stared south towards the graceful curve of the George Washington Bridge.

"It's lovely here! I never dreamed there could be anywhere so like the country in New York City."

They wandered round to the entrance to the Cloisters, and indoors, in the dim stone passages, it was very cool. There were not many people about and there really was something of a monastic atmosphere in the quiet, sun-touched gardens, surrounded by real cloisters.

Drina and Grant were soon separated from the others and Grant quickly showed that he had an eye for beauty and some knowledge of architecture. They looked at Early English and Perpendicular doorways, at delicate fan vaulting and traceries, and examined the many treasures in glass cases. Drina was enchanted with the Unicorn tapestries, particularly with the one of the unicorn captive in a strange little pen.

But she liked the arcades and garden of the Cuxa Cloister best, and presently she and Grant went to stand out in the sun and Grant asked many questions about the ballet and about her own hopes of a dancing career.

Mr and Mrs Chester and Mrs Rossiter looked out at them from the shadows and Mrs Rossiter said:

"What a contrast they make! Your Drina so small and

dark and Grant so tall and fair." She was an observant woman and not unaware of Drina's pleasure in her son's company, but Mrs Chester was thinking about her feet, which hurt after so much walking on stone, and Mr Chester's thoughts were partly still on the Conference, which had been very interesting and informative.

But, though Drina was happy, her thoughts had occasionally gone to Yolande and the evening's show, and suddenly she boiled up into real anxiety again. Where was Yolande and how was she feeling?

Presently they all met again and while Mr and Mrs Chester were occupied in buying booklets and postcards – Grant and his mother helping with their choice – she slipped away to the public telephone. Dropping in the coins and ringing Yolande's number in Greenwich Village, Drina wished quite violently that she had had the strength to stay with Yolande, and yet it had been such a wonderful afternoon. She had been so happy with Grant.

There was no reply and her anxiety increased a hundredfold as she tried again. This time there was a reply: Mrs Dillon herself answered.

"Drina? No, Yolande isn't here at the shop. She was earlier, but she went out for a walk about an hour ago. Have you called MacDougal Alley? Then I guess she's still out. I've had some trouble here. Mamie scalded her hand while making tea for us and she's gone off to the hospital." She sounded rather distraught and Drina hung up feeling worse than ever.

Into her mind came dreadful pictures of Yolande still missing when it was time to go to the theatre. This time it would be a real tragedy, because their names were both in the programme and Madame's alterations would make it difficult for her to carry the ballet alone. Difficult; well, almost impossible. She remembered Yolande's white face and shaken manner on the ship and feared the worst.

But whatever she felt and feared she would have to keep it to herself. The fact that Yolande was out when it was not yet five o'clock would mean nothing to the others, and she couldn't possibly explain. In any case, Yolande might genuinely have gone for a walk and all her fears and doubts be quite groundless.

# 6

# A Ballet in Danger

Drina rejoined the others, relieved that they seemed about to leave. Mrs Rossiter was asking if they would like to go back to the apartment for a cup of tea and her grandmother was refusing.

Drina came to a quick decision and said as casually as she could, "I've just telephoned Yolande, Granny. She wants me to go down to Greenwich Village for a meal before the show." It was a lie, and she hated to be dishonest, but her promise to Yolande bound her. Somehow she *had* to get downtown quickly.

"You'll have to get your things from the hotel," said Mrs Chester, not looking best pleased.

"Yes. Then I can get a taxi down to the Village."

"I'll drive you down," Grant offered cheerfully, and she accepted gratefully, too uneasy now to remember that it might be the last time she ever saw him.

Grant, having no idea that there was any need for haste, took them a slightly longer way round, so that they could have a glimpse of St. John's Cathedral and Columbia University, but at last he dropped his mother in Central Park West and was driving fast towards the Mandeller Hotel.

Drina was only dimly aware of the fact that they had been asked to dinner the next evening, their last in New

York. She almost danced with impatience as they waited for the elevator to carry them to the eleventh floor, and it made it all the worse that she had to hide her impatience from her grandparents.

"Will Mrs Dillon take you both to the theatre?" Mrs Chester asked, as they left the elevator and walked along the corridor.

"Oh, yes, I'm sure she will."

"Then we'll see you afterwards. When is your ballet?"

"In the first half, not long before the intermission. I showed you the programme, Granny. Then we're going to sit in the gallery."

"Very well. We'll see you in the foyer at the end of the show." And Mrs Chester went thankfully to change her shoes, which were by then pinching quite unbearably.

Drina dived for the telephone the moment she was in her room. Perhaps, after all, Yolande was back at the house in MacDougal Alley and all her anxiety had been unnecessary. But still there was no reply and she hastily washed her face, tidied herself and made sure she had everything she would need that evening, including Hansl. It was no good calling the shop again. It was closing time and Mrs Dillon might already be on her way home.

She dashed back along the corridor and waited a long minute for the elevator to fetch her. Grant was still sitting there in the car and she sprang in. The big car moved out into the rush-hour traffic and Grant asked, without even looking at her face, "What's biting you? You're worried about something. What's the hurry to get to the Village?"

Drina hesitated.

"I can't tell you. I promised. But I'm worried about Yolande. I – I've just got to be there to see that she's all right and is going to dance tonight."

She was in no mood to enjoy the drive south, and

Grant was too much occupied with the traffic to talk. But when he dropped her at the entrance to MacDougal Alley he suddenly put his hand on her arm.

"I'm sure looking forward to seeing you dance. And we'll meet again tomorrow."

"Yes," Drina said breathlessly. "I'm so glad – that you're coming to the Carne-Lucas."

But as she rang the bell she wondered if there would be a ballet for him to see.

It was Mrs Dillon who opened the door.

"Drina! What's the matter? Yolande didn't say – "

"Is she back?" Drina gasped, and Yolande's aunt gave her a quick look, then drew her into the hall.

"No. She went out for a walk, as I told you, and since then there's been no sign of her. I must say I thought she'd be back by now, but – "

"It's a quarter to six!"

"Yes, but I guess there's plenty of time. You don't have to be at the theatre until seven-thirty, do you?" And then she gave Drina another very shrewd look. "What is all this?"

"How – how did she seem this afternoon, Mrs Dillon?"

"Seem? Well, I thought she was rather pale and quiet, but I guess she was all right. She's rather a nervy type, but I've thought she seemed much better this week. It's a relief that she likes New York and I'm so happy to have her with me."

"Mrs Dillon, I – I promised and so I can't tell you much. There *may* be nothing to worry about, but Yolande – well, she's very nervous about dancing in public and I – I think I should have stayed with her this afternoon. I'm afraid she may have backed out – "

"And so you've come flying down here without a meal or a rest?" Mrs Dillon asked no further questions.

"Yes. I – I couldn't tell Granny. I said I was coming here for a meal and that we'd go to the theatre together. But if Yolande isn't here I think there's one place where I ought to look – "

"Is it far?"

"Well, not very. Just up Fifth Avenue."

"Go and look, then, and come back here. I'll have a meal ready and I'm sure there's no need to worry."

"But I'd sooner look. I couldn't settle, anyway."

"She'll soon be thinking that *I'm* a nervous type, too," Drina thought ruefully, as she dashed round the corner into Eighth Street. An empty taxi was coming along and she flung herself into it in great relief.

"The Empire State Building, please."

No, it wasn't all that far, but it was – how many blocks? Twenty-six or so. Quite far enough at a busy time. As they drove north she remembered just how Yolande had looked when she had said that the top of the Empire State would make problems seem small.

It was just an odd chance, but it was worth taking for her own peace of mind.

"Only perhaps I'm making a complete idiot of myself," she thought, scarcely noticing the golden evening light, and the great buildings to the north, sharp against the brilliantly blue sky.

She might have been in New York all her life by the way she paid the driver and walked briskly into the Empire State Building. There was no hesitation now, no feeling of incredulity. She paid for her ticket and walked rapidly towards the elevators, and in a minute or two she was high up the great building, changing into another elevator.

There were quite a number of people out on the observation platform and she walked round slowly, looking for Yolande's red head. Dimly she was aware of the vast scene out below, dazzlingly clear now and not partly obscured by mist. The park seemed near and the lakes were blue; the George Washington Bridge sharply spanned the Hudson, and she could even pick out the Cloisters on the heights of Fort Tryon Park.

Long Island, Staten Island and New Jersey were all clear as she walked round; every bridge, every ship, every building seemed sharply marked in the golden light. The downtown skyscrapers reared up, faintly blue in the deepening glow.

It was wonderful beyond words, but she had no time to appreciate it. For Yolande was not there, and she began to realise that she had been foolish to think that she would find her. They might even have passed each other in the elevators or, of course, Yolande might be in the topmost, glassed-in observatory. She went up to see, but there was still no sign of her friend.

She descended to street level, conscious that time was flying, and was once more lucky enough to get a taxi quickly. As she sank down on the back seat she told herself that she was spending a dreadful lot of money, but she still had some dollars left and she had bought nearly all her presents.

The taxi-driver wanted to talk, as usual, and she told him that she had been in New York for ten days and was going back to England on Saturday. He was in the midst of telling her his life story when they reached MacDougal Alley. How attractive the Alley looked in the evening light, but she had no eyes for it. If only Yolande had come back!

But Mrs Dillon, opening the door, shook her head.

"She hasn't come. It begins to look as though she's gotten lost."

Hesitating on the doorstep, Drina happened to glance back up the Alley and there was Yolande, strolling along unconcernedly, with the sunlight touching her hair.

Drina dashed towards her.

"Oh, Yolande, where *have* you been? I thought that the ballet was in danger ... I thought ... I've even been up the Empire State to look for you! I think I've been the most awful idiot!"

# 7

# Curtain Call

Yolande looked astonished and stopped dead.

"But I called – telephoned the shop. Mamie said she'd give Aunt Grace a message."

"Oh!" Immediately it all began to be clear to Drina. "But she didn't get the message. Something happened to Mamie, perhaps straight after your call. She scalded her hand badly and had to go to hospital. I expect it put it out of her head. But where have you been?"

"To have tea with Marilyn. I met her and she asked me. I – I was glad to have something new to think about." And then awareness dawned on Yolande's face. "Oh, Drina, did you think – did you think I'd let you down again? Oh, but I told you I wouldn't. I– I've felt awful, but I'll go through with it. There isn't the slightest doubt about that, though I think I may be sick before we go on."

"Oh, I do hope you're not. Yolande, I'm sorry. I *have* been an idiot! But I telephoned from the Cloisters and you weren't here, and then again from the hotel. I *should* have trusted you, only I kept on remembering – "

" – that night on the ship," Yolande finished grimly. "I was a silly, feeble thing, and I shall never stop being ashamed. Did you have to tell Aunt Grace?"

"Not much. Just that I thought you were nervous. She didn't ask questions."

"She's nice," Yolande said fervently. "I think I *will* tell her all about it, but not until I see what happens tonight."

Then they had reached the house and there were more explanations, though still few questions from Mrs Dillon. Yolande said that she had already eaten all she could, but Drina was ravenously hungry.

"Lucky we aren't on first," she remarked, as she finished up with a second helping of pie and cream.

Yolande grew quieter and quieter as they drove uptown to the Carne-Lucas Theatre, but she did say, as they went through Times Square, where the lights were already shining out and people were hurrying off to evening entertainments:

"Lucky people, going to sit and *watch*!"

"Are you really nervous?" Mrs Dillon asked, and Yolande said quickly:

"Sick with it, but I'll be all right. I'll tell you all about it later, Aunt Grace."

Mrs Dillon left them at the stage door and they went into the long passage that led towards the dressing-rooms. Drina squeezed Yolande's hand briefly. It was very cold, which seemed astonishing and rather alarming when the evening was so hot.

"Yolande, I'm sure it will be all right. Can't you try to enjoy it?"

In the large dressing-room that they were to share with several of the others, Marilyn and the two sisters from Brooklyn were already getting made up. They greeted the new arrivals cheerfully, but Marilyn added:

"I guess I wish it were over. Do people ever grow out of stage fright? *You* ought to know, Drina!"

"Some people never do," Drina remarked, as she laid out her possessions, including Hansl. "Marla Lerieu once told me – "

"Marla Lerieu? The famous British actress? I saw her last year on Broadway. Do you *know* her, then?"

"Well, I've been in two West End plays with her. She told me that she always feels terrible before the curtain goes up."

"Then I guess there's not much hope for *us*. Flowers for someone!" as a messenger came in with a white box.

"For Miss Drina Adams."

Drina took the box, rather startled. Who would think of sending her flowers? Surely not her grandparents?

There was a card on top of the tissue paper and she read it quickly, striving to hide her feelings.

*"Best of luck. I shall be out front. Grant."*

"Orchids!" Marilyn cried, much impressed. "Two. Aren't they just wonderful? I guess no one will send me orchids."

"Boyfriend?" someone asked, leaning over Drina's shoulder.

"She hasn't had time to get herself a boyfriend in New York."

"Ten days ought to be long enough!"

"She met him on the ship," said Yolande, who had caught a glimpse of the card.

"He's just a – a friend," said Drina, hastily putting the orchids in a glass and standing it by Hansl. But her cheeks were bright and her heart racing. How wonderfully exciting life was! Everything was going to be all right; everything *was* all right.

It might only be an amateur show, but the atmosphere of the theatre was all about her. In a short time the curtain would go up and soon she and Yolande would dance. Yolande ... She pushed her own happiness and excitement away and gave her full attention to her friend, who did indeed look pale to the point of sickness.

Make up seemed to make Yolande look worse and, once she was dressed, she sat silent and tense, holding her mascot, a small wooden elephant.

But she followed the others out on to the stage, where the dancers due to perform early in the programme were warming up behind the lowered curtain. Madame bustled up, completely in command of everything.

"All will be well. People are here to enjoy themselves. And, remember, no talking in the wings."

The overture ended and the curtain rose, exactly on time. Standing with Yolande in the prompt corner Drina watched the first item, which was a simple but very charming ballet by the youngest children. And once again, as it had done so often during her first days in New York, incredulity flooded over her.

"This is New York. I'm going to dance in New York. The first time, but it just mustn't be the last." And for just a moment her old fear was with her, that she wouldn't be good enough after all to be taken into the Dominick Company. Now, of course, both Mr Dominick and Miss Volonaise knew that her mother was Ivory, but in the long run, if she herself didn't make the grade, that would be no help. There was always, too, the awful chance that something might happen to stop her dancing. Trouble with her feet, growing too much ... But the latter was so extremely unlikely that she cheered up and divided her attention between Yolande and the dancing children out on the stage.

"All the same," she muttered, as the ballet ended and the next item almost immediately followed, "I shouldn't feel so nervous if it wasn't my own ballet."

"It's a beautiful ballet," Yolande answered firmly. "You ought to show it to them in London."

"Oh, I don't suppose I shall. There won't be an opportunity." And then they both retreated to a corner behind the scenes to get their muscles ready for the coming ordeal.

"Ready?" Madame asked presently. "What is it, Yolande? You look frightened, my child. Try not to worry. If you're to be a dancer you'll have to face far worse audiences than this."

"I know, Madame. I'm all right."

"Then run round to the O.P. side, child. Quickly!"

The familiar music of *Twentieth Century Serenade* began and suddenly, as had happened so often before, Drina was steady and assured. It was too late to worry. Too late for anything but dancing. She moved out into the glare of the lights as Yolande appeared from the other side.

It was all right ... They were dancing. Yolande was dancing well, though her face was still tense.

Drina moved through the dreamy, quiet passages half in a dream herself. Then the music quickened and she began to move with it in a series of wild little pirouettes right across the stage.

Her own ballet ... and Grant out there in the dark auditorium ... faster ... faster ... more pirouettes and then a final leap and turn in the air.

Applause broke out and Yolande had to wait a few moments before she could start her solo. She was relaxed now and suddenly, Drina thought, almost beautiful. She was an ethereal type and the soft white dress made her look even more delicate than usual. She would make a lovely sylphide one day.

Drina's own solo followed and was greeted with even more applause than Yolande's. Then came the final movements of the ballet and the curtain came swishing down to prolonged applause.

Drina and Yolande bowed and smiled and the clapping went on. There were flowers for Yolande (from

her aunt, it turned out), and a lovely bouquet of roses for Drina. Standing there before the curtain, holding them and still smiling and bowing, Drina caught a glimpse of the card, "*From Mr and Mrs Rossiter.*" But it would be Grant's orchids, received behind the scenes, that would be treasured and taken on the homeward voyage.

As she and Yolande retreated for the last time Mrs Rossiter turned to Mrs Chester.

"That other little girl's very charming and a good dancer, I feel sure. But I guess it's your Drina who has the star quality. There's just something about her – the way she stood there, smiling. Anyone can see she's a professional."

"I don't know about star quality," Mrs Chester answered. As usual, and most unwillingly, she had found herself moved by Drina dancing; by Drina holding flowers and bowing and smiling as her mother had smiled. Inherited traits were a very strange thing, and in colouring Drina did not resemble her mother at all, but always, seeing her on stage, Mrs Chester was sharply and painfully reminded of her only daughter, who had been acclaimed by all the world.

Star quality! A great future ballerina. Mrs Chester believed it to be inevitable, little as she wished it to happen. To her there was no escaping the future; a future of endless work and travel for the grandchild she had brought up. And Drina wanted it. Drina sometimes said that she would be more than content to be in the Dominick *corps de ballet*. But it wouldn't stop there. It would go on and on.

Mrs Chester saw little of the solo dances that followed, for she could not get her thoughts away from Drina's destiny.

Drina herself was not thinking about her destiny or

anyone else's. She felt excited and uplifted and everyone else was excited too. There was so much noise in the dressing-room that one of Madame's assistants had to come and restore order.

Yolande, too, seemed relaxed, chattering and laughing.

"Oh, Drina, it's over! I've done it! It will be all right now. And I've you to thank. You might never have wanted to see me again after that awful night on the ship – "

"What rubbish you talk," Drina retorted cheerfully. "I told you – I don't abandon my friends. But I'm glad it was all right, and I'm sure you'll be a dancer one day. And now, if you're ready, let's find those seats in the gallery. I want to see the rest of the show."

Drina awoke on Friday morning to the consciousness that it was her last day in New York. The last time she would see Yolande, the last time she would see Grant Rossiter. *Really* the last time, for tomorrow morning they would sail away.

She spent the morning with her grandparents in Central Park, and in the afternoon she met Yolande and they spent most of the time wandering up and down Fifth Avenue, finally sitting down in the Rockefeller Plaza, under a green and white umbrella.

They had tea and cakes and at first talked hard, but gradually both grew rather silent, for their parting was very near. Yolande admitted to herself how much she had relied on Drina since their curious first meeting on the ship. Without her she would have taken longer to settle to her new life in New York. Drina had been a good friend, thoughtful, sensitive and kind, and Yolande was passionately grateful, but knew no way to express her feelings. It would only have embarrassed Drina, anyway. So she sat silently in the hot sunshine, which had crept under the umbrella, and Drina looked round at the brilliant flags and the flowers, at the golden statue and the wall of falling water, and at the RCA Building soaring straight up into the dark blue sky.

"I do love it. Here especially, but everything else, too. Don't forget to write, Yolande, and do please sometimes send me one of those gorgeous postcards. Send the one of the downtown skyscrapers at sunset, and that one of the United Nations looking so odd against a blue sky – beautiful, really."

"But you've got a whole set. It must have cost you a lot of money."

"I know. But I'd like one or two through the post, with American stamps on them. I know it's silly, but do. And tell me all about the ballet classes and everything that happens to you. You've still got Marilyn. She's a nice girl and she lives near you, and you may be going to school with her."

"She is nice, but I wish you weren't going away so soon."

"I wish it, too. But I suppose I've got to go back and get down to work. I shan't do anything but work for months now. I really must concentrate."

"But things always happen to you. Something else will turn up. Perhaps another part in a play."

"It had better not, then," Drina said grimly. "I've missed nearly a month at the Dominick as it is."

Soon after that she paid the bill and they rose and walked slowly up the steps and along the flower-filled Channel into Fifth Avenue.

"I – I do hope we meet again," muttered Yolande.

"So do I. I'm sure we shall – somehow, someday. I

wish there were somewhere in New York like the Fountain of Trevi in Rome. You drop in a coin and wish and then you're sure to come back. Goodness!" Drina added, laughing, "how Granny would hate to hear me saying that. She loathes me being superstitious. Well, goodbye, then."

"Goodbye," Yolande repeated rather desolately.

"There's a bus. Isn't that the one you want?"

Yolande ran, without a backward glance, and Drina felt very sad, for she always hated partings, and this was far worse than Jenny returning to Willerbury or Rose going off to Chalk Green Manor for three months. But at least Yolande would be all right now. She liked her aunt, was making friends, and surely she would never again get into such a nervous state about dancing in public?

And now – the last evening. Drina went up the escalator to the main lobby of the hotel, then soared to the eleventh floor in the elevator. She knocked at the door of her grandparents' room and found them almost ready for the evening.

In her own room, she ran a bath and sank into the warm water thankfully, for the heat had been as great as usual. Winter might come to New York in a rush, but the beginning of October was still like summer.

Grubbiness and tiredness forgotten, she put on the emerald green dress and her white necklace and ear-rings. A little powder carefully dusted over her brown face ... lipstick? Her grandmother would be cross, but she put on a little and then wiped it nearly all off again. Still, it left an extra touch of colour.

"I almost look pretty, if it wasn't for my funny straight hair," she thought, staring at herself in the looking-glass.

And yet the sleek black hair, swinging so smoothly

round her neck, gave her an air of distinction that no curls could have done.

When it was time to leave she took up her bag and a little white cape and followed her grandparents down to the street.

"It's really very kind of the Rossiters to entertain us so much," Mrs Chester said, as they drove north towards the park.

"Yes, they're very charming and hospitable. Mrs Rossiter said that we mustn't dream of dining in a hotel on our last evening."

Drina said nothing at all, just sat there dreaming, gazing out at the scenes that were already familiar. Sunset light lay over the city and, looking downtown as they left the taxi, she saw that lights were springing up already in the great frieze of buildings south of the park.

It seemed, as they sat at the Rossiters' table in the big dining-room high above New York, that it couldn't be the last time. That soon, so very soon, New York would be nothing but a dream – something in the past.

"But I shall be different because of it," she thought, watching Grant and remembering Yolande and all her other experiences. "Some of it will go on."

When they had had their coffee Drina asked if she could go and look at the lights and wandered away into the big room at the front. She stood there by the open windows, staring at that miraculous view, and suddenly found Grant at her side.

"Did you ever go up the Empire State or the RCA at night?"

"No," she said, rather sadly. "There wasn't time, somehow."

"Well, look here! Why don't we go now?"

Drina turned towards him in the dark room.

"Just you and me?"

"Yes. Just the two of us. I'll fix it."

Drina followed him back into the lighted dining-room, astonished and elated.

# 8

# Drina Sails Away

Mrs Chester looked startled when she heard the suggestion.

"It's very kind, but I really don't think – it's after half-past nine already and I think that Drina still has some packing to do."

"She can sleep for a week on the ship," said Mrs Rossiter, moved by Drina's look of wild hope. "And, besides, it wouldn't take long. They can go down in a taxi; it's hardly worth getting out the car. Grant is very responsible and he'll look after her."

"I'll bring her right back here," Grant promised.

"Let her go," Mr Chester said to his wife. "It will be a wonderful sight and it *is* her last night in New York."

Drina grabbed up her bag and cape and she and Grant went down the elevator. She was so happy that she hardly knew what to say, but as it happened Grant talked to the taxi driver as they drove towards Fifth Avenue.

The Rockefeller Plaza was ablaze with lights and she cried, as they encircled the Lower Plaza on their way to the front of the RCA Building:

"I love this almost best of all! I wish I could skate here in winter."

"I often do," he said. "Do you like skating?"

"I love it, but actually I don't often dare, because I'm so afraid of getting a sprained ankle or anything like that."

There were few people about in the great building and they were the only two in the elevator. Drina reached the top with slightly singing ears and followed him out to the observation platform. New York burst on her as she went forward – millions of glittering lights below and far away. It was a very clear night and the streets and buildings, the bridges over the river, the lights of Brooklyn and Queens, the Bronx and New Jersey, had a jewelled sharpness.

She grasped the parapet and stared and stared, so moved that for a long time she couldn't speak.

"I've seen a lot," she said breathlessly, presently. "It's nearly all been wonderful. But *this* – oh, *thank you* for bringing me!"

"Come round to look south," Grant said, and put his hand on her arm to draw her round the dark and almost deserted platform. That way it was even more wonderful, for not far away was the fairy tower of the Empire State Building, the beacon light swinging round, and, far below and to their right, was the coloured blaze of Broadway, unmistakable amongst the other, darker streets.

"I think it must be the most beautiful city in the world!"

"I guess not many would agree with you," he said dryly. "It's the fashion to say it's noisy and ugly, garish and vulgar. It can be all those, but I – well, I'm a New Yorker. I think there's nowhere like it."

"There *is* nowhere like it, I'm sure. I do think that New York is truly beautiful. *Look* at that! I – well, I'm always feeling that things can't be real. It's a dream. I shall think so tomorrow, when we've sailed away. But I

shall never forget, never.''

Grant looked down at her face, just visible in the light from an open doorway.

"You'll have to come back."

"I mean to. Oh, I do mean to. But I may be grown up by then."

"How old are you now?"

"Fifteen on November 1st."

"In a year or two," he said carefully, "it's quite likely that I'll spend some time working in London. My father's firm are thinking of starting a branch there. Give me your address and some day perhaps you'll come to Covent Garden with me."

"Oh, I should like that! And to the Dominick."

"You may be dancing there then, I guess."

"I shan't even be a senior student until a year next September. We – I – no one knows now who'll be rejected."

"You'll be chosen," he said with certainty. "You're just a kid, but I'm sure you're really good. Anyway, remember. One day I'll turn up in London."

"I'll remember," Drina promised, and turned away to hide the tears wobbling on her lashes. As they spread all the glittering lights blurred and merged, but it was happiness and not sorrow that was making her cry.

Soon afterwards she looked her last at that superlative view and followed Grant to the elevator. It was nearly over, but now she could be philosophical about it. It was the end, and yet not quite the end, for a thread, perhaps very tenuous but still real, bound her to Grant and, through him, to New York. For she did not think he was basically a casual person and some day she really might see him again.

The next morning Drina stood alone on the Boat Deck

of the *Victoria* as she sailed down the Hudson River. It was a vividly blue morning and every building was sharp and clear, every detail of the city she had so soon learned to love etched in the sunshine.

Soon they were past the downtown skyscrapers and she looked back, standing there staring, staring as gradually even the highest buildings disappeared behind the nearer structures on Long Island.

But soon they showed again, and she continued to see them, a blue frieze against the sky, for a long, long time.

Then, at last, she sighed and turned away, to go down below to A Deck and start her unpacking. New York had gone, was over, and she must turn her thoughts towards the Dominick again, and all her friends. To Ilonka at "The Golden Zither," to Rose amongst the autumn beechwoods of Chalk Green, and to Jenny in Willerbury.

And when she reached her cabin she found several letters waiting for her, addressed to the ship. She took up Jenny's first.

*When you read this*, wrote Jenny, *you'll be on your way home. And how great it'll be to think of you back in Westminster, on the other end of the telephone. I expect it was wonderful. I expect that, just now, you're feeling sorry it's over. But think of all your friends.*

*I do miss you, and you must try and come for a weekend soon. We shan't be moving for a while yet, so do come while there's still plenty of room.*

*But if you come I'm afraid you'll have to come farming with me on Saturday and Sunday. You needn't do much: just wander about elegantly collecting eggs or something. I've got a job at weekends on a farm outside Willerbury. My uncle got it for me; he guessed how I was feeling. They're very short-handed and it gives the farmer's wife a rest and me a breath of life. Besides, it's a way of earning some money.*

*So now I can put up with the school and that awful book-keeping quite cheerfully, with milking and mucking out and the rest to look forward to all week. It will count as experience, too, if I ever do get to an agricultural college.*

*Enjoy the voyage and ring me up just as soon as you get back.*

*Much love,*
*Jenny*

"Oh, I'm so glad!" And Drina felt a little cloud roll off her heart. Jenny farming at weekends was a hundred times better than Jenny enduring book-keeping and shorthand and thinking of a future office job.

"Are you ready, Drina?" asked her grandmother's voice, and Mrs Chester stood in the doorway. "Well, leave your unpacking until afterwards. It's lunchtime."

Drina followed her obediently, feeling the faint motion of the ship. She would have plenty of time in the coming week to get her thoughts in order, and there might still be interesting new experiences.

# DRINA

Follow Drina's fortunes, from her first ballet lessons to her triumphant appearances on stages throughout the world, in the popular Drina series of books.

| | |
|---|---|
| Ballet for Drina | £2.99 ☐ |
| Drina's Dancing Year | £2.99 ☐ |
| Drina Dances in Exile | £2.99 ☐ |
| Drina Dances in Italy | £2.99 ☐ |
| Drina Dances Again | £2.99 ☐ |
| Drina Dances in New York | £2.99 ☐ |
| Drina Dances in Paris | £2.99 ☐ |
| Drina Dances in Madeira | £2.99 ☐ |
| Drina Dances in Switzerland | £2.99 ☐ |
| Drina Goes on Tour | £2.99 ☐ |
| Drina, Ballerina | £2.99 ☐ |

*All Simon & Schuster Young Books are available at your local bookshop or can be ordered direct from the publisher. Just tick the titles you want and fill in the form below. Prices and availability subject to change without notice.*

Simon & Schuster Cash Sales Department, PO Box 11, Falmouth, Cornwall, TR10 9EN, England.

Please enclose a cheque or postal order to the value of the cover price and allow the following for postage and packing:
UK: 80p for the first book, and 20p for each additional book ordered up to a maximum charge of 2.00.
BFPO: 80p for the first book, and 20p for each addition book.
OVERSEAS & EIRE: £1.50 for the first book, £1.00 for the second book, and 30p for each subsequent book.

Name ......................................................................................

Address ..................................................................................

.............................................................................................

Postcode ...............................................................................